To Janet

Hope you enjoy reading my book

Olga

THE JINXED SHORE

BY

OLGA BEATTY

THE JINXED SHORE

ISBN 1 85863 021 5

First published 1993 by

MINERVA PRESS
2, Old Brompton Road
London SW7 3DQ

Printed in Great Britain by
B.W.D. Ltd. Northolt, Middlesex.

THE JINXED SHORE

He was weak-kneed but resolute as he looked at her still ashen face and said, "I am not your plaything Mary, when you feel like it, but I will lay my cards fair and square on the table. If you can say to me now, in all honesty, that you don't love McGready, I will call off my wedding".

She looked at him with red rimmed eyes, disappointed that he had mistaken her need of comfort for being a deranged mistress, then unable to bear the interrogation of his eyes, as he waited for her to forsake Shaun, she turned her back on him.

She heard him gulp the last of the drink, put the glass on the table, then the click of the door as it closed behind him.

*****

Olga Beatty, 5th child in a family of eight was born and brought up in Omagh, County Tyrone. While juggling the demands of a family of four with assisting her eldest son in running a wine importing business she went back to college in Teesside and was encouraged by her English tutor to take up writing. When life became less hectic she decided to give it a try. What better setting for her first novel than the beautiful Donegal Coast where she and her husband, Ian, spent many summers in holiday cottages with their children. She now lives in Cambridge and makes frequent visits to Donegal and her home County in Northern Ireland.

To the most wonderful mother in the world:

Jeannie Wilson

Chapter One

The locals eyed her with curiosity as they made their way back from a day's shopping in Letterkenny. An elderly gentleman joined the bus at Dunfanaghy and took the vacant seat next to her. She remembered her mother telling her about how friendly the people were in these parts, verging on nosiness, as he struck up a conversation straight away, laying his walking stick between them.

"Stranger in these parts then?".

"Yes, I've come to visit my aunt".

"Ah, and who would that be?".

"Katie McGrath!". He arched his bushy eyebrows quizzically as if he didn't understand her English accent. She fumbled in her handbag and drew out the card with her aunt's name and address on it and held it out to him.

He reached into his pocket and pulled out his spectacle case. It took him a few minutes to focus on the print having to hold his hand out the full length of his arm. His eyes lit up with recognition as he exclaimed, "Katie McGrath! So she's your aunt, is she?". He turned and looked at her keenly. "Aye, by gorra, sure I can see the resemblance now. There was another one of them - went off in strange circumstances. You'd be her daughter then?"

Mary didn't want to enlarge on that, it wouldn't be proper

to tell a stranger about her mother before Aunt Katie so she asked him if she could get a taxi when they arrived at Falcarragh. He laughed as if he found the idea of it ridiculous and said, "You should have arranged that yesterday!".

Her worried look was apparent and he immediately said, "Ugh, sure it's only a wee dander for a young'un like you. Don't worry, I'll set you on your way".

He started to reminisce, "I was at school with your grandfather. The capers Kieron and I got up to in those days would make your hair stand on end. One night Kieron laid his hands on a gun and we went off shootin'". Her eyes widened. "Not people! Aw naw, not people; nor pigeons either, we wern't daft. We shot all the lights out in Dunfanaghy. Ah, Jaysis, sure those were the days".

Mary lowered her eyes. She hoped her Aunt Katie didn't take after her father.

"You'd be a lady then? Pampered looking you are. What part of England do you come from, Miss?"

"I'm from...". The bus pulled in.

He joined in the gibbering Irish chatter with the locals as they got off the bus, then he drew her aside, "It's a fair wee dander now, a mile I'd say. Just take that road up yonder and keep goin', you won't miss Katie's as there's only the Lodge and the Manor out that road".

She shook hands with the man and thanked him before

walking in the direction he had indicated.

Aunt Katie didn't know she was coming. Maybe it was a blessing that the telephone line had been blown down in the storm because she might not have wanted her to come. They lived life at such a slow pace in this remote part of Ireland that to be cut off occasionally was looked upon as a blessing. "Miss McGrath said she was in no hurry, but we hope to have it working by the end of the week", the telephone engineer had said.

Thankfully it was a pleasant day for walking and although wide enough for cars, the road couldn't be regarded as much more than a track. She had heard quite a lot about Donegal over the years from her mother but she had never suggested taking her there because of the row she had with her sister. Ulster consisted of nine counties, the three counties Donegal, Cavan and Monaghan were independent of the other six.

The views were simply breathtaking from this narrow road winding upwards and inland. There was a wild grandeur with occasional scenic glimpses of the shore beyond the lush green fertile valleys. The sheep grazed contentedly in the sweeping pastures on each side of the road where she knew they were grown for wool rather than mutton; hence the well known Donegal knitteds.

She walked a considerable distance before stopping for a rest on a little grey stone bridge. She looked over into the clear water of the stream and became fascinated by the little fish. Hurriedly she made her way to the other side of the bridge and climbed over the stile then knelt down to look into the crystalline water. What a beautiful aquatic sight: Minnows! Hundreds of them, swimming past in the slow flowing water, shoal after shoal, every plant and stone clearly visible.

The unpolluted, clear water reflected a spectrum of colours in the sunlight. Each minnow seemed to gleam and produce its own light. Why, there were so many of them she should have no trouble catching a whole handful. Cupping her hands together she reached into the water - they all slipped through her fingers, with the exception of one. The little minnow leaped and squirmed for dear life, in fits and starts. Her artistic eye for colours, forever alert, observed it. It was green along the back and silvery, with a violet blue tinge along the sides and thin greyish feathery gills.

"Don't worry little minnow!", she murmured, "I'm going to set you free; but at this moment I have an affinity with you. Our security has been badly disrupted and neither of us knows what lies ahead; we are between the devil and the deep blue sea".

She lowered her cupped hands into the water and the little minnow lept free. It weaved in and out through the clumps of fine plants and frog larvae until it caught up and mingled with a shoal. She watched the shoal go down stream. Would it never, like herself, take the good things in life for granted again?

She stood up, brushed her clothes with her hands then climbed back over the stile and headed up the road again. 'Mother, has your soul arrived here yet? Do you know if that little minnow has calmed down after its ordeal?'.

Mary had lived in the West Heath district of Birmingham all her life. She had heard that her mother and father left Ireland as there was very little employment in Donegal. Oh, how her mother had loved it here in Falcarragh, she always spoke of it with a dreamy, far away, look in her eyes. It must have been a bad row for her never to set foot back in this lovely place. Yes, she paid a tragically high price when she made the decision never to see her sister again.

There was not a lot of money to spare, but at the same time she never wanted for anything. There had been ample to cover the funeral expenses with a reasonable amount left over. The building society account named Mary jointly with her mother as she had been one for keeping her affairs in order.

Mary found this trip extremely inconvenient and expensive to say the least, but she had to get it over and done with for her mother's sake. She felt a tremendous sense of grieving as she recalled sitting by her mother's bed in the hospital.

"Am I going to die today, Mary?", Sue asked weakly.

"Of course you're not! You're going to get better".

She took no notice of Mary's answer as she whispered, "Tomorrow then, or maybe the day after". She closed her eyes wearily.

Mary was in no way *au fait* with the unfamiliar situation and felt at a complete loss. She turned her mother's hand over in hers, even that was unrecognizable as the flesh had fallen off it over the past weeks. Her mother would very likely pass away that day but she had to be strong and not communicate her anxieties. She had no immunity and did not respond to the treatment for the acute microbial infection that had released the powerful toxins and devastated her body.

Sue hardly ever mentioned her sister. If she had spoken of her half a dozen times in Mary's lifetime, it would have been the height of it. That day for some reason her sister was very vivid in her mind.

Her voice, that came in fits and starts, due to the respiratory condition that had developed, was determined to carry on. "Oh, how my sister and I used to enjoy playing on the beach at Dunfanaghy. Our mother and father used to walk hand in hand laughing and joking to each other in the Irish tongue. It was the first language, English was only spoken for the tourists".

"Oh, Mother, the doctor's won't be pleased at you blethering on, I was told to keep you quiet".

"Why, Mary? Sure I'll be quiet soon enough".

She lifted her head off the pillow as best she could and her voice became exuberant as she spoke, "I have no worries about leaving you, Mary, because you have been blessed with beauty and brains. My sister wili look after you, it's her turn now. I don't want you to be sad about me dying either, you see, although my body will be laid to rest here in West Heath, my soul will be going home to join Matt's".

Mary wished her mother would stop ranting and raving; she wasn't so sure about her soul but her body was getting weaker by the minute. She tenderly stroked back her light brown hair, streaked with grey. Although in her forties, she was a very attractive woman and had the power to catch the roving eyes of men. Their eyes lingered on her longer than necessary, but she never held a gaze; always kept it to a glance, more often than not avoiding their eyes completely. Her whole life revolved around Mary and no amount of persuading could have changed her ways.

Her eyes looked into Mary's as she said, "I want you to deliver a letter to your Aunt Katie in person. If she is adamant in not opening it, I would like you to dispose of it".

"But, mother...".

"Please, Mary, will you promise to do as I ask?". Mary had never seen such irritable pleading in her mother's eyes.

"If that is your wish, mother, then I will go to Donegal and deliver the letter to your sister. My reservation is that if she didn't want to see you, why on earth should she want to see me?".

"Oh, she'll want to see you alright, Mary, you see...". She seemed to be in pain and laid her head back on the pillow, then gasped, "in my bedside drawer...".

Before Mary had time to call the nurse her mother had slipped into unconsciousness and a guiding light had gone out on Mary's world.

A thatched cottage suddenly came into view as she got round the bend. It stood in a large, well stocked garden bordered by small fields. She unlatched the gate and walked up the path; the bag she was carrying seemed to get heavier with each step and she hoped her aunt was at home. The front door was wide open and a little long haired dog ran towards her and gave one bark.

"Hello!", called Mary.

"If you are looking for the Manor", a voice called, "It's a hundred yards further round the next bend".

Mary became totally rooted to the spot: her mother had retained her Irish accent and it was almost as if she had heard her calling to her from the grave - or was it her soul? When the voice came into view she was further shocked; if she had not buried her mother a few weeks ago she would have sworn this woman was she. She hadn't expected the resemblance to be so striking even though she knew they were twins, she had her mother's colouring and was of the same height and build.

The woman observed, at first glance, the immaculately dressed young woman in the pale blue suit and white blouse and couldn't fail to notice how pretty she was. Mary had been blessed with curly brown hair that behaved itself and had a good clear skin.

"You must be Aunt Katie! I'm Mary Lavery", she said in a voice hardly above a whisper.

The woman was outwardly stunned and looked her straight in the eyes. Aye, sure the eyes told it all... After a timely pause she extended her hand in an embarrassed fashion and said, "Come in and sit down, you will be tired after the exhausting journey and having to carry that bag all the way out here".

She led her through to the living room. It was only when Mary sat down did she realize just how very tired she was. The little dog made friends with her by licking each of her hands in turn.

Katie wasn't one for showing her emotions and tried to hide her excitement as much as possible but a little tear got the better of her and she dabbed at her eye with the end of her apron.

She tried to pull herself together. "What brings you here child?", she asked.

"My mother died two weeks ago", said Mary as she rummaged for the letter in her handbag. "I would have tried to find you sooner but I had to vacate the house and see to her belongings".

Mary handed over the thick envelope. Katie was very pale from the sudden shock and held onto the edge of a chair to steady herself.

"This is dreadful news!", she said as she lowered herself into the chair fingering the envelope nervously. "I am very sorry for you my dear, you must be devastated".

"It happened two weeks ago on Thursday", Mary choked back a sob, unable to keep her self-control any longer. She was suddenly tinged with fear; her safe little world had been shattered and the gravity of it all was only beginning to have an impact.

Katie immediately got up and went to Mary and gave her shoulder a pat, saying, "You have had an awful ordeal child and you'll never know how glad I am that you came here. Stay as long as you want".

She went back to her chair and after a suitable interval, she asked, "What on earth caused her death at such a young age".

"It was a rare type of infection; I can explain it in more detail but it's very technical. They brought in consultants from other regions, but there was nothing they could do for her".

Mary looked at Katie and felt sorry for the blow she had just dealt her and said, "My mother mentioned you from time to time over the years, but when I tried to probe she always changed the subject. I only know that you both had a quarrel and she seemed to want to forget all about it and for me to know as little about you as possible, so for her sake I let my curiosity fade".

"I'm sorry, I can't forgive your mother and no letter", she

eyed it anxiously, "after all this time is going to make the slightest iota of difference. You won't have heard the story and I'm not going to be the one to tell you, but I can tell you that I have not set eyes on her since your father died twenty years ago. I went to the funeral to pay my respects to Matt, a good friend of mine, but I wasn't invited to the wake. My only regret that day was that I didn't see you", said Katie with a quiver.

"I don't know what happened between you both, but mother, certainly at the end, would have liked to patch things up. She had the letter written for some time, I don't know if she ever intended to send it to you, I only know she was adamant about you getting it, especially when she thought she might die", said Mary and then went on to deliver her mother's message regarding the letter.

"Very well", Katie replied to the request, "I'll sleep on it for a while but chances are you will get it back to dispose of it", she said as she stuffed it into her apron pocket.

"How about a nice cup of tea and a home baked scone, we can both be doing with it?", offered Katie.

"I'd love that, thank you", replied Mary, thinking she would have plenty of time to question her later.

While Katie was making the tea Mary noticed how very charming the cottage was with period features, dark wood panelling walls and inglenook fireplace. It was the first time she had ever been inside a place like this and she felt a remarkable sense of homeliness as she relaxed into the chair while the little dog settled contentedly at her feet.

Katie came back with the tea and Mary drank thirstily. She interrogated Mary on her earlier life and listened attentively to every word she uttered. She wanted to know so much about her without making too much reference to Sue.

Mary had a reasonably happy childhood, but being an only child spent a lot of time with her mother. She was a dressmaker for as long as Mary could remember and was perpetually busy. Mary was always well turned out, almost all her clothing was made by her mother and very few items were bought off the peg.

To pass the hours when her mother was sewing she played around with paints and after a while developed quite a talent. She had started off sketching simple still life; a sunflower to begin with, colouring the petals with a mixture of bright yellow, burnt orange and gold and the centre a mixture of orange and black pigment to produce brown. It wasn't long before her efforts were displayed on the wall at school. When her mother realised this she encouraged her to paint more and more. "My sewing proved a godsend so perhaps you can take up painting later on in life".

Mary felt a bit of an outcast at school and resented the other children who had lots of relations. She used to fantasise that her best friend, who lived close by, was her sister.

She took a degree course at the University of Aston in 'Office Management and Technology with French' and Sue was delighted when she was awarded a First. "Much as I would like to see you settled into a career, the world is your oyster, so take your time and give it a good deal of thought", she had told her.

Unfortunately Sue was struck down with the illness, so serious decisions had to take a back seat.

Katie never tired of Mary's past revelations and threw question after question, it was akin to trying to pack twenty two years into an evening.

"I really am delighted that you came and I meant what I said about staying as long as you wish. Forget about job hunting for the moment, you will need time to get over the shock".

That night Mary sat in the guest bedroom and tried to absorb the events of the day. Only this morning she had set out on this inconvenient chore, she was now overwhelmed by it all. Her eyes filled with tears as she thought of her mother whom she missed so much and the aunt who seemed to dote on her already. "I must do something, somehow, for Aunt Katie to make up for whatever happened years ago, that deprived her, and us all, of each other's company".

Mary and Katie spent a thoroughly enjoyable first day together. Katie excitedly gave an account of her life as they worked cheerfully, side by side. She was an outdoor person and had about 100 barn reared hens which just about kept the neighbourhood in eggs. She also ran a small market garden business, selling vegetables, flowers and fruit, especially strawberries. For the past three years, with local help, she had grown a unique type of strawberry, with a delicious flavour, that gave good yields right through from May to October, by staggering the planting. She also sold rare herbaceous plants and shrubs that she had propagated and was able to establish a good little by-line to make a reasonable living when the hens took a rest from laying.

Mary knew that her mother and Katie had been only seventeen when their parents had been killed in an automobile accident on a railway crossing near Londonderry and had to carry on as best they could. They lived in a typical country fashion in those days, managing on four goats, a dozen chickens and half a dozen rows of potatoes and carrots. Her mother romanticised the slow paced past but sometimes contradicted herself with the true remembrance of its terrible harshness.

Katie told Mary that she held the tenancy of the cottage but it belonged to the owner of the Manor. "I wouldn't want to live anywhere else on earth, it's such a peaceful and tranquil place to be, the people in the village are a caring lot and everybody here knows each other".

Mary assisted Katie with the washing and grading of the eggs then loaded them in trollies in readiness for collection. She then kept herself busy in the house while Katie finished feeding the hens.

They settled down in front of a blazing hearth in the evening. Katie had been cut off from the joys of having a family, and sitting opposite this girl, she relished the warmhearted sensation of sharing and contentment.

Mary was tired after the day's physical exertion. She closed her eyes and said softly, "I never knew there was such a wonderful place on this earth; I love it here Aunt Katie!".

Katie looked across at her peaceful face, flushed from the warmth of the fire, it was obvious the area had made quite an impression on her. The weight of responsibility lay heavily on her shoulders; she had deprived the girl for years of her rightful homeland in Donegal.

Chapter Two

In the days that followed Mary enjoyed herself enormously. In comparison to town life there was so much to enjoy. The delights seemed endless: unpolluted air, open spaces, green grass, clear rivers, deserted beaches, beautiful countryside and amazing wildlife, not to mention the fresh fish they had in abundance which were caught locally.

Mary was riding Katie's bicycle back towards the Lodge after shopping in the village, when she was startled out of her wits by a big silver car coming round the bend. She wobbled all over the road before falling off. The driver had already stopped when he saw her start to wobble, he jumped out quickly and helped her to her feet saying harshly, "My god, I could have killed you! You tourists are all the same; you come here with the impression that no one uses these roads and that they are only here for your benefit?".

She listened to the gist of the remarks and said in embarrassment, "I'm sorry, I got carried away looking at the lambs over the hedge and forgot myself".

He gripped her shoulder roughly and said, "The last thing I want to do is kill off a young member of the fair sex, so if you are going to ride around these roads in safety you will need to be more vigilant!"

He picked up her bike and inspected it for any damage, then asked curtly, "Are you alright?".

"Yes, thank you", she answered, then jumped on the bike, wobbled past his large car and rode off. With the wind on her back she free wheeled when she got over the breast of the hill. Raising both her arms high in the air, her words echoed piercingly as they blew over the fields, "To hell with good looking, opinionated, patronising, overbearing, filthy rich and high falutin' men..."

She was too embarrassed to mention the episode to Katie so put it to the back of her mind.

The following Tuesday morning as Mary was brushing her hair, a car drew up at the front door and a man got out and walked briskly up the path. She looked more closely through the net curtains and her heart thumped as she realized it was the same person she had the unfortunate encounter with on the road.

She heard Aunt Katie invite the man in then went off to collect his eggs. Mary didn't want to go down until he left, but her aunt was such a long time she decided to go and see where she was.

She was just trying to nip out of the back door when the voice said, "Hello! Oh, it's you again!".

"I'm Mary, Katie's niece, I'll just see what is keeping her".

"Ah, now that you have a name, can I introduce myself also. I am Ron Casey from the Manor", he said as he stood up extending his hand.

"How do you do", said Mary putting her hand in his.

"I thought you might be staying with Katie, but as a tourist on holiday. I hope you are none the worse for your mishap the other day and perhaps I should apologise for being rude, I have a short fuse when it comes to ignorance of our roads".

He asked how long she would be staying in the area and she answered, "I'm not sure, perhaps a few weeks".

"You are in for a pleasant holiday, the scenery and tranquillity are unimaginable".

"Yes, I'm thoroughly enjoying the glorious scenery, riding around on Aunt Katie's bicycle".

"I take it your aunt's bicycle is still intact then", he quipped. Their eyes met in a smile, she looked away hastily, he disturbed her somewhat.

"Yes, thanks to you managing to come to a halt so quickly".

"What do you do for a living then, when you are at home?" he asked.

"Nothing yet. I have just graduated and am in the process of deciding what to do with my future. I have a few pointers going in different directions, I don't want to be in too much of a rush to settle on one in case I deny myself the others", replied Mary.

"Very good thinking - what are you best at?".

She was bored with his questioning and wished he would mind his own damn business. "Oh, nothing in particular".

"I hope an answer like that doesn't mean you will hide your light under a bushel".

Katie came in hurriedly and handed Ron a tray of eggs, "I see you two have got acquainted. When Mary sets eyes on the Manor, she will be wanting to paint it".

"Goddammit, a decorator too is she?", he goaded with a smirk. "I'll be delighted to show you round the Manor and grounds tomorrow evening. I will collect you both at 7 O'clock for dinner".

He left before Mary could conjure up a plausible excuse. As she watched him drive off, she said, "I can't stand presumptuous people. What does he do for a living anyway?".

"He is a workaholic loner who has little time for tact or diplomacy but he grows on you. I'm very fond of him now. He has become very rich as a property developer and bought the Manor and grounds, which consisted of twenty five acres, about three years ago. He then sold off twenty two of the acres to the local farmers who had rented them and retained the Manor and three acres of gardens. He apparently started in a very small way but has since gained acçolades for his hard work and does a lot for charity. The Manor is among his hundreds of enterprises and he has restored it beyond recognition. Because of the character and position, he has had six bids for it and up to the present has turned them all down. I believe he has a soft spot for it but I wouldn't be surprised if he lets it go one of these days".

"Oh, so he isn't local then?", Mary asked.

"When he first came about the place he said his father had worked in these parts, but I hadn't heard of him".

All her life Mary had been a town-dweller but she settled in to the countryside like a duck to water. She was willing to help Katie in any way she could. Today she took the front garden to task, removing the dead flower heads of the marigold and Californian poppies, to lengthen the flowering period and pulled out all the chickweed. She stepped back, taking off her gardening gloves and observed her handiwork, admiring how colourful the geraniums looked; mixtures of white, pink, blue and purple.

Ricky the little shi-tzu decided, as Mary had finished gardening, it must be time for a walk so he started to wag his tail and jump up and down. She gave him a pat and called, "Won't be long Katie, just going down to the stream to give Ricky some exercise, he's getting fat lying about the garden".

Katie had brought her down to this little stream yesterday afternoon and already Mary knew she was going to miss the beauty of it all when she went away. She perched herself up on the tree trunk and wondered how often her mother had sat here and bit into her lip as she thought, Oh Mother, why? We could have spent our holidays here, instead of trailing off to those overcrowded commercialised seaside resorts.

After she had a good brood, she called, "Come on Ricky, race you back". Just as she jumped down she became aware of a grey haired, thick set man gazing at her from the other side of the stream.

"Don't look so alarmed", he said, "My name is Kevin Casey, father of Ron who owns the Manor. When I saw you sitting on the tree trunk it was almost as if I had gone back in time as you are so very uncannily like someone I used to know and come here with. You're Katie's daughter aren't you?", he surmised.

"No, Katie is my aunt, my mother's twin sister".

"I assumed you were Katie's daughter as I seem to remember Sue moved to England. Indeed it's been such a long time since I've visited these parts that I thought Katie would probably also have moved. How is your mother keeping, by the way?"

"My mother is dead", said Mary, and went on to explain the circumstances of her death.

Kevin seemed visibly shaken by the news and said, "I am very sorry to hear that. What a shame for one so young to be left without a mother and father. Your father and I were very good friends, his death was a great shock to me".

"I never knew my father, I was only two when he died", said Mary. "He had an alcoholic condition. My mother never blamed him for that, she said it was a disease over which he had no control".

"Oh no! Indeed he had his first drink in the company of myself and a few of the lads. He was unfortunate to have a genetic tendency to alcohol and his bouts of drinking were triggered by environmental stresses, the everyday social pressures that the average non drinker can cope with. Yes, it was a great tragedy when it came to that", said Kevin.

Mary found it difficult to speak of her father, a man she never knew, so she changed the subject.

"Ron has invited us to dinner tonight, I do hope you will be there", said Mary. She had taken an immediate liking to the man.

"I arrived unexpectedly this morning and he did say something about having guests to dinner and that I should join them. What a coincidence, Katie McGrath and I meeting up again after all these years! Perhaps I shouldn't intrude on your evening. If I had known I would have stayed away until tomorrow", said Kevin.

"I'm glad you came today, Kevin. I am looking forward to meeting you again tonight".

"Has Katie any family of her own?" Kevin asked quietly.

"No, my Aunt Katie never did get married, surprisingly

enough", responded Mary.

Kevin answered in a constrained voice, "What a shame", then went on to make a request, "Mary, could one stranger ask a favour of another stranger? You see, I would very much like to surprise Katie tonight".

"I won't say a thing, I hope it's a nice surprise".

"I hope so too", said Kevin as he moved off.

Mary hadn't the slightest idea what to expect tonight, if she had been invited properly she possibly would have refused as she had hardly a suitable stitch to wear until her clothes arrived from home. The only clothes she had was the suit she came in and one dress which wasn't exactly evening wear and a few casual clothes such as jeans and tops.

She stood in front of the full length mirror for a final appraisal. In the circumstances she looked quite well, she thought. The pale blue cotton dress with its simple lines flattered her figure. Mother insisted on adding a crisp white collar and slim white belt and that set it off nicely.

She pulled on a pair of white peep toe shoes and transferred her comb and lipstick into her white bag.

"I'm not one for going out", said Katie as they waited for Ron, "But I'm dying to see how Ron decorated the dining room. Last time I was up there, he talked about pulling down the old fashioned lights and replacing them with chandeliers".

Katie looked particularly nice tonight in her well cut floral patterned dress and short jacket. She had blow-dried her hair into a casual style and had added a little touch of make-up and pink lipstick. Mary couldn't believe how alike Katie and her mother were, she even had the same fussy mannerisms. She was fiddling around checking, more than once, that she had everything. Meeting Katie definitely softened the blow of losing her mother. If it wasn't for Katie continually asking questions regarding her past, she could almost forget her mother was dead.

Ron announced his arrival by giving a sharp toot of his horn. He was tall and lean in comparison with his father, she thought, with dark hair and sharp features. He was casually dressed and looked quite dashing in a blue denim shirt and casual khaki well tailored trousers with a brown leather belt. The blue shirt complimented his tan and made him look exceptionally handsome. Oh, how she hated handsome men, they always thought they were God's gift to women and the bee's knees.

"We have an extra guest for dinner tonight. My father arrived unexpectedly this morning. His nosiness got the better of him, I didn't think he would stay away much longer. He is a building contractor and couldn't wait to see what I had done to the old dilàpidated building that he used to frequent in his young days".

A magnificent Manor came into view around the bend. Mary admired the setting as she stepped out. She particularly liked the hedging which gave the Manor its seclusion. Ron followed her gaze and said, "They are a particularly nice type of conifer, aren't they? They are called 'Thuja plicata', I have been informed by John the gardener. He chose them ten years ago, they should grow a good deal taller over the years".

The gardens looked super, so mature, Aunt Katie had made an accurate assumption when stating that she would want to paint it. She would love the chance to settle her easel there one fine afternoon.

As they entered the hallway, an oversized friendly looking middle aged woman rushed up to meet them. "This is Alison, John's wife, who I have already mentioned to you. She has been housekeeper and has run this house admirably for years before I came on the scene and is the best cook in the County".

"Oh, don't listen to that banter, if it wasn't for Katie's fresh vegetables and eggs, not to mention the strawberries, I'd just be mediocre".

She told them their starter was on the table and to go ahead into the dining room.

Katie entered, ahead of Mary, in cheerful anticipation. She stopped dead in her tracks when she saw the grey haired man standing by the hearth. Their eyes met.

"I'd like you both to meet my father", said Ron. "First of all this is Katie, who lives in the Lodge down the road, and keeps me up to date with all the goings on in the neighbourhood".

Kevin smiled cautiously, "No need to introduce Katie, I told you I once lived and worked in these parts. I am very pleased, and surprised, to meet you again Katie. I never dreamt you would still be living in this part of the country". His voice had deepened, become more mellow over the years.

Katie pretended not to see the outstretched hand and said in a low voice, "Hello, Kevin".

"Now meet Mary, Katie's niece, who is over here on a visit", said Ron.

"We met very briefly down by the stream today. Nice to meet you again, Mr Casey", said Mary politely.

Oh, if only Mary had mentioned that she had met him today, this confrontation could have been avoided, Katie thought. He was the last bastard on this earth she wanted to see, she was sure Ron had said his father's name was Ken, come to think of it he could have said Kev.

The bastard could have taken himself off elsewhere when he knew I was coming - he knew she hated him so he had long since stopped trying to see her. In the end she had to revert to sending him a solicitor's letter to stop him hounding her. He moved away after that and she hadn't seen him again until now. One of her friends, Lucy Watson, told her he had started up his own building business, after being an architect for years and that it was on the up and up, "flourishing", she had said. He looked like a man who had made it, he had always been a man of great presence, now superseded by a more laid-back look, calm and composed. The rat has got even more handsome in his maturity, she thought. He was of medium height with broad shoulders, his waistline had thickened over the years but he looked extremely fresh for his age. I wonder how many more hearts the damn bugger has broken? To think that she had been within a hair's breadth of marrying him. She had put his devastated reaction to the split down to anger and hurt pride rather than unrequited love.

She was on tenterhooks with this fate-worse-than-death phenomenon. There was one thing he was good at and that was concealing things, Ron doesn't seem to know a damn thing about his past. He had a catastrophic effect on her and she hated him for making her put on an act tonight, as she didn't want to ruin everyone's evening.

She looked towards the ceiling and drew attention to the chandeliers which looked absolutely magnificent. "Yes, it took three day's work to get those monstrosities into place", Ron laughed proudly.

Kevin went off to get the chilled wine as Ron seated them around the table.

The meal was delicious; seafood scallops, combined haddock, mushrooms and shrimps caught locally and served on the natural scallop shells, followed by chicken in celery sauce. Alison had prepared a magnificent cider syllabub, decorated with Katie's home grown strawberries for the sweet.

Kevin and Mary hit it off particularly well and shared

quite a number of amusing stories.
Ron told them all about his forthcoming venture of taking over a château near Paris, with the intention of transforming it into luxury flats.

Later Alison showed Mary and Katie over the Manor, disclosing that Ron had fallen in love with it at first sight and the price had been fantastic. It had been in a dilapidated state but with his superb foresight and business acumen he knew it could be a good investment.

There were many delicate well proportioned rooms with beautifully polished carved wood mantlepieces. The library had a massive columnar chimney-piece, the walls decorated in hand painted wallpaper.

The bedroom/study that Ron occupied contained a four poster bed, Alison informed them that it was eighteenth century. The four poster was draped in cream taffeta, with a frill around the top falling from deep rows of smocking. On one wall stood an eighteenth century bureau cabinet with a rounded top to the fitted writing drawer. The leather covered writing surface could be drawn forward from under the pigeon holes to offer more space and allowed access to a shallow well of papers. This lid was controlled by a pair of knob handles composed of segments of mahogany. An antique Baccarat sulphide paper weight with a huntsman and dog set into the translucent green glass took pride of place on the bureau. There was a matching wide upholstered seat with richly carved legs and carving on the arm ends to match the bureau.

Another wall was taken up with books, video and stereo equipment and the polished oak floorboards were complemented by a large Persian rug.

As they came back into the drawing room they heard Kevin say, "I suppose you will put the place on the market now that it is restored". Ron's reply was, "Not necessarily, I've become quite attached to it and I have to live somewhere, why not here?"

"There's a lot to be made on this Manor with it's beautiful peaceful setting. I gather you have had quite a few offers already?", remarked Kevin.

"I have done well enough out of previous ventures, so money isn't the main object any more. I may decide to cut out the weekend work and enjoy the beauty and tranquillity that this place offers".

"That'll be the day, I can't see you exchanging the life you lead in the fast lane just yet; a chip of the old block", chuckled Kevin proudly.

Kevin was having a short break from work since his doctor had diagnosed angina. Apparently there wasn't a lot they could do for him except prescribe tablets to help the pain. The cardiologist told him to learn to live with it, take care of his diet and with a reasonable amount of exercise together with a bit of luck thrown in, he could live into old age. He hoped to be back in the thick of it next month.

They all contributed to some light hearted banter, then

Ron said, "Mary, lets take a walk in the garden, you will be pleasantly surprised at how well John looks after it and we will give father and Katie a chance to get acquainted again after all these years."

Katie gave Mary her jacket which she had taken off and told her to put it over her shoulders in the cool evening air.

The garden looked magnificent as they stepped into the deepening twilight. To the rear of the Manor, was a massive expanse of artistically planned flower beds. Mary loved gardening which had been just as well as her mother simply hadn't the time. This one was expertly planned and actually would not take a lot of looking after due to the care taken when planting.

Ron showed great pride in the gardens. "John, our gardener looks after all of this and does a marvellous job. I'm afraid I am no gardener, I can just about differentiate between a rose and a daisy, I simply admire and enjoy".

He guided her to a part that had been left to nature. One could enjoy the peace and the profusion of wild flowers that had sustained beauty. There was just enough light left in the sky for her to make out lady's bed straw, salad burnet, bee orchid, milkwort, cowslips and quaking grass. She noticed an area of herbs among a selection of flowers and as she came closer was aware of the mixture of aromas. The chives were at the stage of flowering, past their best for eating. She stooped and plucked off a blue flower, saying, "Planting highly aromatic plants such as mint, rosemary and garlic, repulses the pests and discourages them from attacking nearby plants".

He led her up a little cobbled path in the direction of the summer house, it was quaint and blended in with the overhanging trees. "I can understand your love for this place and your wish to remain here, it is a splendid setting".

"I am certainly going to hold onto it for the meantime as a base. My office is in London and I also own a flat there but it is lovely to get out into the countryside."

Next he guided her down a path beyond the summer house, through the laurel bushes to a magnificent waterfall running down massive rocks. This area of the garden had well placed spotlights, the main beam softened by foliage. Mary was spellbound, it really was enchanting.

Ron stopped and faced her. "By the way have you given any further thought to your future?", he asked.

"No, I'm afraid not. I have been fully occupied enjoying myself".

"Don't hesitate to ask for my assistance if you think I can be of any help. I am perhaps a bit more worldly wise than yourself or Katie".

Mary looked closely at him, the lights silhouetted his form; this man was too damned attractive, she wished he didn't effect her the way he did. She thanked him and said, "If Katie had her way she would like me to stay here".

In response, he spoke quickly, "Don't let her persuade you to do that, I think you have real potential, you are bright and intelligent, the one that employs you will be the winner. From my observations, Katie has wasted her life. Don't let her do that to you!".

Her eyes became conspicuous and animated in the illuminated beam. There was something about them, almost as if he was accustomed to them. She had a natural beauty and a magnetic lure but still innocent enough to be impervious to it. He didn't know what possessed him to touch her, it was an unsolicited impulse he couldn't resist, his fingers closed around her arm just below her sleeve cuff. Touching women wasn't one of his regular pastimes, but when he did, the message was conveyed straight away. With Mary, he could feel her flinch at his touch and let her go as a cat scurried between them.

She had found his gaze and touch embarrassing as she had no experience of dealing with men not to mention one of such attraction and stature. Her eyes had implored him to touch her, but when he did, her body couldn't deal with it. Episodes such as these seemed to have the opposite effect on her and made her aware of her inexperience and inadequacy. It could have arisen from her mother's attitude to men, she always turned the other cheek when flattered or pursued by them. Mary likewise refused to go out with the boys from the college, there was no one she felt ready to get involved with. Sally, her friend, thought she was barmy to turn down some of the offers she had. "Next time John Turner invites you out, point him in my direction, he is a real hunk", she had said with amusement.

"I'll accept, for the meantime, that you are a 'look but do not touch' type of girl", murmured Ron as they made their way back.

As they approached the house Mary tried to get on to a lighter note by saying, "I am very fond of your father, we seem to have a good understanding already although we have only met".

"I'm glad you like him, Mary. We were separated from each other for years as he was divorced from my mother since I was a baby. She wasn't keen on me meeting up with him: When I was fifteen I persuaded her to let me get in contact and when we eventually did meet up, he told me about the hassles he had over the years as he tried to persuade my mother to let him see me. My step-father, Jack, was very good to me, I cannot fault him in any way. I love both of my fathers dearly".

Katie seemed relieved to see them and said, "I think it is time we were off, my girl, I have been told that Kevin and Ron are catching a flight to London tomorrow and will have to make an early start".

"Yes", said Ron, "Airports are few and far between in this part of the country, we have to drive into the North and get a flight from Aldergrove".

Kevin stood up and said, "It has been a pleasure meeting you, Mary, I hope I have the opportunity to meet up with you again".

"Indeed I hope so, Kevin", she said enthusiastically.

Kevin and Katie bid each other an unpretentious goodbye.

Ron ran them both home and as Mary got out of the car he said, "While I am gone, feel free to do any sketching you want in the grounds. I will tell Alison and John to very probably expect you".

"Thank you, I might just take up your offer".

"I hope you clinch your deal in London with Monsieur André Pierre", Katie called lightheartedly.

That night when Mary was undressing she thought of Ron's phrase, 'for the meantime' and became enlivened with an unprecedented zing. She was falling headlong into the trap she had hoped to avoid.

As they drove past in the morning Ron stopped off to deliver Alison's weekly market garden order for Katie. As he left, he said to Mary, "I hope you are still here when I come back. I would be delighted to show you some of the beautiful sights of Donegal".

"Oh, that would be nice, thank you. I hope I'm still here then". He laid his hand lightly on her shoulder as he said goodbye. She smiled and didn't flinch.

Katie said goodbye to Ron inside, but Mary went out to wave them both off.

Chapter Three

Kevin sat quietly in the car as they made their way along the road towards the Airport. He recalled his embittered confrontation with Katie the previous night when they were left alone. She was as beautiful as ever, the lines around her eyes simply added a new dimension to her beauty and her figure had filled out in more rounded curves. All the desire of old had come flooding back as if it had never gone and he had to conceal it as best he could as she started into him with a barrage of words. "If you think you can worm your way back into my life you are far mistaken. I shook the dust off my feet many years ago and I never wanted to see you again. Never!". The old animosity for him still engulfed her and she was intent on keeping the vendetta alive. "I will keep up appearances when Ron and Mary are here but don't ever expect me to be pleasant to you when we are on our own", she had said with bitterness.

There was no way that he and Katie could ever be harmonious again, it had been a monumental error of judgement to expect harmony. Therefore he had said to her frankly, "Alright, we have both suffered, I at your hands and you because of your narrow minded, sanctimonious, unforgiving attitude. It was a long time ago and a lot of water has run under the bridge since. I suppose it was just too much to expect that you would have put the long-term irresponsible antisocial behaviour behind you. I can assure you, categorically, that if you were the last person on this earth, I wouldn't touch you with a barge pole".

She had flushed with anger, she didn't like being put in place with a flea in her ear. Not another word passed between them until Ron and Mary came in.

He never dreamt that Katie would still be living in the cottage when he decided to make a surprise visit on Ron. He thought she would have married years ago as she was a beautiful woman. He never bothered her after she had the solicitor's letter sent to him. If a woman took that stance, then she must have hated him.

If it hadn't been for Katie he wouldn't have come on this trip with Ron. He would have stayed around for a few days and maybe had a game of golf at his old club. When Ron asked if he would like to join him he thought perhaps it was best to extend the miles between himself and she.

Ron's words broke into his thoughts, "Katie's niece, Mary, seems to be a delightful person. It's strange she has never visited previously".

"There was a silly row between the sisters apparently, but I can't remember much about it", said Kevin.

"I'd like to get to know her better, that is, if she will allow it, she is a bit stand offish, not in an unfriendly way, perhaps just inexperienced and cautious".

"I'm proud of you son, and in many ways you take after me; but hopefully you'll be luckier in love than I was. An innocent young girl like that shouldn't be pursued too quickly, I think you should take your time and if you are lucky enough to ever gain her affections, for God's sake, deal with it better than I did. I made a mess of my love life, and at the end of the day, it's all important".

Ron glimpsed sideways at his father and wondered what wisdom his words harboured.

The following Tuesday Mary took delivery of two packed trunks dispatched from Mrs Thompson, a very kind neighbour at West Heath. Regrettably she knew it was time she was making tracks. "Regardless of where you go Mary", Katie said sincerely, "I would like this to be your home to come to whenever you feel like it".

Mary was overjoyed as she reached over and kissed her aunt's cheek, "I only wish circumstances had been different and that we had all met up sooner".

"Well, luckily, we can make up for those wasted years now" ventured Katie contentedly.

Mary registered with some London agencies for secretarial work and hoped they would find something suitable very soon. She unpacked her easel, folding-stool and gathered together her sketching equipment and headed towards the Manor with Ricky following closely at her heels.

Taking her time, she chose her spot fastidiously. After she got the angle right, with just the right amount of light and shade, she settled down to sketch. She started to draw in the general shape of the Manor using a mixture of ultra marine and burnt umber with sable and worked a warm wash into the sky area using light red and yellow. She then worked in the distant tree shapes. To accentuate the sky warmth she added a blue and white distance, using broken brushwork.

Presently, John, the gardener, appeared from behind the hedge and Mary observed his coarse weather-beaten face and large rough hands. He spoke with a timid muffled Irish accent, "Alison say's you're to go in when'er it suits you. The kettle's puffin' away. We're actin' on orders from Ron to look after you", he grinned.

She decided to walk back with John, stopping occasionally to admire or ask the name of a plant. She asked him how he had managed to have such a spectacular range of lilies, he told her he had grown them from seed and then took great pride in going into detail on how he had succeeded with them. He had covered the bottom of a deep container with broken crocks and grit, adding a compost and fertiliser. After he had sown the seeds, he left them outside for two years, covered with glass in the winter, then potted them till they were ready to plant in the garden.

Alison met them at the door and said, "His lilies are his pride and joy, I hope he didn't bore you about how he grew them from seed".

"No, on the contrary, I'm honoured to have been told", she smiled.

Over tea and scones Mary learned that Alison and John had worked together at this job for twenty five years. "It was good in the old days when the house was alive. We were kept busy then. Since Ron took over we haven't really worked to full capacity, he comes and goes, only occasionally bringing the odd visitor. It is mostly a matter of keeping the place presentable now, I'm afraid".

"Did you know my mother?", Mary ventured cautiously.

"Yes", replied Alison, "I knew your mother".

"How much do you know about what happened between my mother and Katie?"

"I'm afraid I knew very little, so I can't help you. It was all so sudden you see, not even Matt knew what happened between them in their own house. The wedding was cancelled at short notice and Sue dragged Matt off and they got married quietly elsewhere and never set foot in the area again".

"So nobody knew what happened between them?", murmured Mary unbelievably.

"Rumour has it that Katie got cold feet at the last moment. Sue was livid at the idea of her leading Kevin, who was besotted with her, up the garden path and they had a bad fall out and both were too proud to make it up. It didn't wash with John and I, but who knows. One often wonders had their parents been alive if the whole sad incident would ever have transpired".

"Kevin who?" urged Mary, she had never heard that Katie had been contemplating marriage.

"Why, Kevin Casey of course".

"My God, she wasn't going to marry Kevin, was she?", retorted Mary astonished.

"I think you need to have a word with Katie, Mary, I seem to have said too much already", replied Alison.

This explains why Kevin and Katie weren't over enamoured with each other and it also explains Kevin's request for her not to mention he was going to be present for dinner. Oh, I wish I had known, thought Mary.

She became aware that Alison was talking, "It was a big surprise for me to find out that Kevin was Ron's father and a mind-boggling experience that Katie and Kevin were meeting up for dinner that night. Then I heard Ron making the introductions so I assume he doesn't even know yet that they were once to be married - Oh I have put my two big feet in it this time".

"No harm done, Alison, don't worry about it", uttered Mary.

Chapter Four

Mary arrived back at the cottage in the early evening to find Katie busy making the little bedroom to the back spick-and-span. She said, "I hope you don't mind that I have accepted a visitor this week. He is a scenic artist and has stayed quite a few times in the past. If it had been anyone other than Shaun, I would have put them off".

"Of course I don't mind - I'll move into the small room and let him have the larger one".

"No need, he always requests the back room", replied Katie. She went to great lengths to make this visitor seem as nondescript as possible, probably because she felt guilty about taking a booking while Mary was a guest. "He won't arrive until late and he is making an early start towards Innisfree Bay in the morning. He is a very quiet person and no trouble at all, you will hardly know he is here and should see very little of him".

Shaun McGready was a quiet spoken man in his thirties from North of the border. He had rugged good looks with tousled grey speckled brown hair that fell across a scarred forehead.

"Is painting your main occupation ?", Mary asked out of curiosity over a nightcap of milky malted drink.

"I make a very good living out of it now, but painting isn't usually one's career choice, I suppose in a way one is either lead into it as a diversion after having made it elsewhere, or driven into it as a necessity when all other avenues are closed".

"Do you fall into one of those categories?", queried Mary with interest.

"I fall into the latter, I had a bad experience and it created a turning point in my life. Donegal is one of my favourite haunts for painting with its deep glens, winding bays and rugged cliffs. It has scenery unsurpassed for wild grandeur", Shaun ventured with a soft faraway look in his eyes.

"Mary paints, she has already made a start on the Manor", exclaimed Katie proudly.

"Oh, just a little, nothing special, perhaps some day, like yourself, I shall take it up more seriously", Mary replied with embarrassment, "I put some entries in a few exhibitions at my previous college. The other students liked them, but they probably wouldn't be good enough for a public exhibition".

"Well, you are welcome to come out with me tomorrow. I am heading towards one of the many beautiful bays and will be making an early start", he said.

Katie looked towards Mary with encouragement, "Shaun is one of the best in his field, a well known lecturer on oil, watercolour and acrylic painting techniques to the privileged few, you shouldn't miss such an opportunity".

"Well, think about it, if you would like to come, just be up and about before eight in the morning", said Shaun as he bid them goodnight.

"Are you sure you won't mind Aunt Katie, I really should be giving you a hand".

"Much and all as I appreciate your help, I did very well before you arrived and I'll do very well after you've gone", assured Katie. "No, you go off with Shaun, he is the most reliable, not to mention amusing person, one would ever hope to meet. I'll have your breakfasts ready early and give you a call before I go out to deal with the hens".

Shaun was already sitting down at breakfast when Mary came down stairs. "Good morning, isn't it a lovely day? Pack your shorts as it could get hot and sticky today", he said.

"He must have wormed his way into your good books, Aunt Katie", remarked Mary, as they both followed him to the car, "Here you are packing me off for the day with a complete stranger".

"Ah, you will find out about Shaun, he is the salt of the earth", beamed Katie.

They drove to the edge of the sea at Bunbeg, Innisfree Bay and parked the car in the sand dunes. Mary had never seen a beach like it for its massive expanse of silky golden sands. "This part of Donegal is known as 'Bloody Foreland' because the sun, particularly during the summer months, turns the rocks to a reddish shade which can be both beautiful and eerie", Shaun told her.

She excitedly flung off her sandals and ran to the edge of the water and paddled about happily like an invigorated child.

Shaun watched quietly from the distance as he unpacked his gear and felt compensated already for having asked her on the spur of the moment. It had been out of character for him to get saddled for the day with an amateur, except for the times he took the art classes.

The area had a natural beauty that even bureaucrats and developers would be hard pressed to ruin. The bay's perfectly smooth sands and numerous nooks and crannies attracted tourists but not on a grand scale. One could still enjoy the tranquillity of it all. Mary thought to herself, when the sun is shining here, who would want to be anywhere else on earth.

She discovered, over the course of the day, that Shaun was very fastidious when it came down to serious work. His standards were high, his expectations exacting and his complaints loud if the demands he made on her were not met. He demonstrated some of the fine techniques which had brought him such acclaim both in Ireland, England and further afield. Mary hadn't seen his TV series, that had run so successfully in Ulster, but Aunt Katie had told her last night that he had a massive following. He was keen to encourage all would-be-artists from absolute beginners to undiscovered masters.

He described his own work as depicting the rain, the mist and the wind. "I want you to think that your boots are sodden and your socks squelching, the feeling that you're right out in the middle of it", he mused.

"In landscape painting don't place the horizon line too near the centre of your panel. A general rule is two-thirds sky to one-third landscape, or one-third sky to two-thirds landscape. Rules can always be broken so long as the subject matter is of sufficient interest. Work some warm lights into the sky, then place the reflections into the water. Always keep the surface of the water simple". One could see he was in his element painting as he thought aloud for the benefit of the student.

They thoroughly enjoyed Aunt Katie's splendid lunch and he made sure it was a leisurely affair and wouldn't be trapped into talking shop. He was an incredibly interesting man, laughed heartily when disclosing childhood pranks, then just as suddenly his face would convey a sadness as if conscience-stricken at his pleasure.

As he stood up he asked her if she had the stamina for another session. "I am quite happy to let you have a relaxing afternoon to yourself, if you don't feel up to it", he said giving her the choice.

"If you can put up with me, then I'm definitely keen to keep going".

"You have great potential as an artist you know. You just have to learn to throw some of your bad habits out the window". He then added, "Your mother was a remarkable woman in recognising that you had talent, some poor devils have a talent that lies dormant due to lack of encouragement".

Shaun took some photographs so that they could put the finishing touches to it at a later stage, this was his usual practice allowing him to get on with a different scene the following day.

"I have enjoyed your company today", said Shaun on the drive back, "I hope you feel it was worth it and that you have picked up a few tips. I won't have time to coach you tomorrow as I have the television crew trailing around in the afternoon and my morning will be taken up in preparation for them. We will have a further session the following day, if you wish?".

Mary didn't know how to thank this man for his kindness, "You really don't have to drag me around with you".

"I want to! You are a breath of fresh air and I can indeed be doing with some of that at the moment. It's a lonely game painting and it's not easy to get someone to share it with that has just the right amount of balance between work and relaxation. With the exception of my chiding today we hit it almost right".

"It has been one of the most enjoyable days I have spent for some time and I would love to accompany you again", said Mary, delighted.

Shaun went off before Mary was up in the morning. She and Aunt Katie had a leisurely breakfast. Mary enthusiastically talked about the previous day. Katie was delighted that Mary and Shaun had hit it off.

"Shaun was a school teacher, he had taught history and geography, until he and his eight month pregnant wife were involved in a horrific accident six years ago. A loaded crate fell off the lorry they were following and flattened half the car they were in. His wife was killed instantly and Shaun suffered severe injuries and was concussed for days, hence his slight limp and scar."

Mary had noticed his slight limp but didn't ask, as she thought it was maybe something he was born with.

"His injuries caused him to take a year off school, but he decided not to go back after that as he got hooked on painting, which had, up to that point in his life, just been his hobby. He never dreamt that he could make a living out of it", continued Katie.

A blessing in disguise, thought Mary, then retracted it, when she thought of the wife and baby he had lost.

Mary kept herself occupied that day helping Katie with the cleaning of the barns and had another bash at the painting of the Manor. She decided to start again from scratch making use of the lessons of the previous day and the difference was striking.

Next day Shaun and Mary headed off in the direction of Portnablagh and Marble Hill. The rugged coastline along this stretch was softened regularly by a succession of beautiful beaches, with golden sand and clear unpolluted waters. The paintings of this area must surely take pride of place among the connoisseurs' collection.

Two more educational days in Shaun's company brought them closer together. Mary marvelled at the Irish, they were such accommodating and genuinely friendly people. The general atmosphere was one of open-handed hospitality and relaxation. In a very short time she had made such fantastic friends.

"I'm going to miss you, Mary, when we part", he said sincerely as they made their way along the beach at Maghery Bay on the last evening. He put his arm around her shoulder and pressed her to him and she instinctively intertwined her arm around his waist and they walked contentedly towards the car.

Katie and Mary saw Shaun off next morning. He was going further down the Donegal coast to Bundoran where he was putting on an exhibition of his work including 'The Wishing Chair' and 'The Fairy Bridge', these were two areas of coastal rocks in the Bundoran area that had been configurated into bizarre shapes by the brisk Atlantic winds.

"Don't forget to write to me my girl and let me know your whereabouts. Just a little bit of work on those paintings and you will have them ready for exhibiting. I have a booking in Dunfanaghy in a month's time, I will try and get permission to squeeze them in there", he said.

Katie waved him off and Mary blew him a kiss. He stuck his head out of the window and shouted, displaying a grin from ear to ear, "I'll be wanting a proper smacker next time not a blown one".

"I must give you credit Mary for bringing life back into that face", said Katie, "It seems no time since he sat and cried buckets in my house, saying, "The good Lord got it wrong Katie, he should have taken me, not Maria and the baby?"

"Oh, I am so sorry for him, he must have been destroyed", said Mary sadly.

"Don't think about it Mary, he has built a new life for himself and will be happy again", said Katie. "By the way, my friend Lucy and I have tickets for a country concert tonight. We booked the seats about a month ago, if you are interested in country music and would like to join us, perhaps if I rang around, I could lay hands on another ticket".

"Yes indeed I am fond of country music but I think it's time I got down to a bit of letter writing. You two go off and have a great time and enjoy yourselves", urged Mary.

Lucy arrived at 7.00pm to collect Katie and after waving them off Mary settled down to write a letter of thanks to Mrs Thompson, who had taken everything in hand at the time of her mother's death. She also wrote to her best friend Sally and told her that she missed her and that they would have to meet up again as soon as possible. 'It is impossible to describe the rugged scenery here and hopefully I can invite you for a short stay after I get sorted out' she had written.

The phone rang in the middle of her trend of thought.

"Hello Mary, it's Ron here, I'm so glad I've caught you in".

"Hello! How are you?", said Mary in a surprised voice.

"I'm in a bit of a quandary, Mary, I am depending on you to get me out of my predicament", said Ron quickly. "My secretary can't speak a damn word of French and I need to clinch a deal the day after tomorrow. I haven't time to advertise for an interpreter so I'd like you to get a flight to London early tomorrow".

Mary sniggered under her breath. How like a man, what he really meant was he couldn't speak a damn word of French himself. "I can't do it, Ron, at such short notice, surely you can get someone from an agency", she suggested.

"I want you, Mary, I haven't time to get used to someone new. My secretary will make all the arrangements. She will ring you first thing in the morning and let you know what time the taxi will be calling for you. I'm in a desperate hurry now, I'll have to go".

"Wait, Ron, how long am I going to be needed for?", she asked swiftly, "And what ..?", but the line went dead.

My God, what a bully, thought Mary. He never gave her a chance to ask what type of clothing she would need to take.

Katie invited Lucy in for a coffee after arriving back late from the concert. There was a note on the kitchen table from Mary. It read 'If the phone rings early in the morning, please don't disturb yourself, it will be for me. I am going to London, and possibly, Paris. I will explain all later'.

Lucy was an old friend of both Katie and Sue, right back from school days. She married Jock Watson and was the mother of two sons and the proud grandmother of three. Now in her mid-forties she was a well padded homely woman with a heart of gold. She had kept in touch with Sue for a short time after the breakup, but after Matt's death Sue stopped writing to her. Lucy was disappointed as she always hoped she could bring the girls together.

"It would do you the world of good to get a break, Katie, and you know I am only too willing to keep things ticking over for you here", she said, making a fuss of Ricky as he stood on his hind legs leaning on her knee.

"That'll be the day that I'd be jetting off to London and Paris", laughed Katie. "No, I am too set in my ways and don't yearn for things like that".

"Well, keep my offer in mind and think it over for another time. Even a few days in Dublin would do you the world of good and I'd have a great time here spoiling Ricky".

"Thanks, Lucy, I know you mean well and I will indeed keep it in mind", said Katie unconvincingly.

Mary was up with the lark, she had so much to do. She decided against jeans and tee shirts as she didn't think she would have any leisure time and packed her best clothing. As she was in the shower the phone rang and with a towel wrapped around her she answered it.

"Hello, is that Mary Lavery, Mr Ron Casey's niece speaking?", the officious young woman's voice asked.

Oh, that man has such cheek, Mary thought furiously to herself and answered tolerantly, "Yes, speaking".

"This is Karin Bonnington, Ron's secretary. I have arranged for a taxi to pick you up at 9.30am this morning. Your flight ticket can be picked up at Aldergrove Airport from the Britannia check-in desk. Your flight time is 1.30pm and Mr Casey will be meeting you personally when it arrives in at 2.30pm.

Mary thought it best to make no complaints or comments and thanked her.

"Mind you don't stay a day longer than is necessary. They have a damn cheek those Caseys and would walk over you if you'd let them. I can remember that Kevin one of old and they are birds of a feather".

Katie has changed her tune since she discovered Kevin was Ron's father, thought Mary, it's not long since she had sung his praises. Mary knew she was going to eventually have it out with Katie about why she didn't tell her she had ditched Kevin, when almost at the alter, but it needed a diplomatic approach and she was too hassled at the moment.

Ron smiled broadly as Mary stepped through the arrivals exit. She didn't reciprocate and immediately hurled a torrent of words at him, "What in Heaven's name do you take me for, I've known you for such a short time but you already have me dancing to your tune. I'm a novice as far as what you want me to do is concerned, I won't do your company any good you know".

"You'll be marvellous, don't worry. I'm taking you straight to my flat in Kensington to wind down", he said, "I have all the papers and documents needed for tomorrow's meeting therefore there will be no need for you to go to the office. We have a lunch time meeting at the Hilton with André Pierre at 12.15."

Ron's flat was the height of luxury. She sank down into the plush peaches and cream upholstered suite and closed her eyes. This was Heaven after all the upheaval. First the rush to get out with Aunt Katie fussing around just like mother, then the dilemma of the delayed flight causing her worry in case Ron would be agitated. As it happened, because he was calm and collected she retaliated in a filthy mood by flying off the handle.

When Mary opened her eyes she discovered Ron standing outlined against the window, thoughtfully observing her. "You are so refreshingly lovely in a sublimely innocent type of way. That look can't stop one having itchy fingers though".

Mary lowered her eyes in case he would see the stupid

yearning she had in them for his touch. This man disturbed her from the first time she set eyes on him. Perhaps she was dazzled by his reputation - or very likely it was a delayed school-girl-crush. She had always been shy in the company of the opposite sex due to being smothered by her mother. Yes, she thought, in no way would it be natural to crave attentions from someone as overbearing as Ron Casey.

"I haven't booked you into a hotel for the night, you can stay here with me, it will save my chauffeur time in the morning as he is only a block away", said Ron.

Mary was about to protest at the idea of them sharing a flat when the door opened and in walked Kevin. She stood up immediately and extended her hand for his handshake.

"Mary, I am so delighted to see you again, it's marvellous that you were able to make it", proclaimed Kevin as he took her hand in both of his and held unto it. "I overheard Ron on the phone asking you in a 'bull in a china shop' sort of way and I felt you would turn him down".

"I wasn't given the chance to turn him down, I was bamboozled into it", smiled Mary.

"How have you been keeping?", Mary asked cordially.

"Oh, well enough, a bit tired though, I'm not just as able as I was some years ago at burning the candle both ends".

Ron showed Mary to her room so that she could freshen

up before going out to eat. "Jenny, my cleaning lady when I am in residence, has prepared the room for you", said Ron. Mary looked about her with intense observation, the decor was gracefully finished in cream. "This place is magnificent", remarked Mary, and must have cost the earth, she thought, as she had read about the exorbitant prices of flats in London.

"Cost a pretty penny too", hollered Kevin from the hallway, "Wait till you see what he is trying to buy in France when you go the day after tomorrow. I had the pleasure of doing the survey for the château a month ago and I can assure you it is magnificent."

"I have to ask you yet if you will be willing to come with us" Ron said, as Mary gazed questioningly. "I have both you and Kevin booked on the flight with me, but it may never happen unless the meeting goes well tomorrow and I can negotiate a good price".

"I don't think I'll eat out with you both tonight, I'm feeling a little tired. I'll make myself a sandwich and have an early night if you don't mind", said Kevin as Ron entered his bedroom.

"I thought you were getting dressed", said Ron.

"Well, I came in to dress but decided to have a rest on top of the bed and must have dozed off, so off you go and enjoy yourselves and I'll see you both in the morning".

"Are you sure you're alright, father, you look a bit pale and seem to be constantly out of breath?", asked Ron.

"Of course I'm alright, nothing that a rest won't put right, so off you go".

When they got outside, Ron decided that they would walk to a little restaurant which he frequented. "They have the best steak in town", he said with enthusiasm.

The head waiter came forward immediately and said, "Mr Casey, I am honoured to see you again. Please come this way."

He showed them to a quiet table almost surrounded by foliage. Ron thanked him and asked for the wine list. Mary was enjoying this immensely, she wasn't in the habit of eating in such luxurious surroundings.

"I am assured of this coveted seat when in the company of a beautiful woman. If father had been with us or a business partner he would have given us a good central position".

"Indeed", said Mary nonchalantly with a shrug of her shoulder, "I suppose you often sit at this table then?".

"Not as often as I would wish", replied Ron with a taunting smile.

Ron left a hefty tip with the waiter and bid him goodnight after having thoroughly enjoyed a terrific meal.

The waiter bowed to Mary and said, "I do hope you will dine with us again".

Mary smiled and Ron quickly said, "Indeed I am hoping so".

"Well, did you enjoy your summer pudding with Chantilly cream?", Ron teased Mary as he put his arm around her shoulder when they stepped outside.

"It was delicious, you don't know what you missed", replied Mary as she leaned against him.

It was still twilight so they walked for a short while and as Mary had only been to London on one previous occasion she asked if they could have a short trip on the underground. They took the Circle Line changing to the Northern Line and got off at Leicester Square. As they walked around a freelance photographer took their photograph together. Ron paid for it and without looking handed it to Mary to put in her handbag. He had enough of the crowded streets so hailed a taxi to get them back. As they sat in the taxi Mary produced the photograph. They both laughed at it before she put it back in her handbag, Ron had his hand in the air as if to wave away the photographer and Mary was clinging to his arm smiling happily.

After they paid off the taxi and approached Ron's flat Mary said, "Thank you for this evening, I thoroughly enjoyed everything about it, the restaurant, the meal, the underground and Leicester Square".

Ron turned to her as they stepped inside the porch and said "I'm glad you enjoyed tonight because tomorrow we have a full day which can be very tiring when you are not used to it. At 9 O'clock in the morning my chauffeur will be collecting you to take you shopping for whatever clothes you need for this business trip and will have you back at the flat at 11.15 prompt. As I told you previously our lunch time meeting is at 12.15".

When they stepped inside Ron handed Mary a message that was by the phone, it simply read 'Mary, ring Katie'.

"Feel free", Ron said gesturing to the phone as he picked up his brief case and straight away sorted through some notes on the Château De Montville.

He couldn't help overhearing the one sided conversation. Mary said, "Oh, Shaun?"

"Did he indeed?"

"That is marvellous! Tell him that is fine by me and I will ring him as soon as I get back".

Katie was obviously doing a lot of talking as it seemed an age before Mary said, "Bye, Aunt Katie and stop worrying about me, everything is just fine, I will ring you each day".

"Who is this Shaun that the message was obviously from?" pried Ron.

"Oh, just someone I met", replied Mary.

"It isn't McGready, the crippled man with the ugly scar by any chance, who most of the time wears filthy clothes?", he went on sarcastically.

"Yes, the one and same man" exploded Mary defensively, "How can you be so hurtful about a man who has been through so much. He has an almost undetected limp, same goes for his scar, as for his filthy clothes, they are indeed filthy some of the time but only after a hard day's painting and come to think of it, I love those filthy clothes".

"You and I are not going to hit it off, are we? That is the second time today that you have had to let off steam at me. Looks like we are incompatible and the sooner we get this little episode over the better for both our sakes", he said grabbing her elbow while stuffing a wad of notes in her hand.

Her eyes widened in disbelief; she dropped the notes and they scattered all over the floor as she faced him furiously, "You filthy swine", she said, "You needn't think you can buy my favours with all the money in the world, I hate you and I'm going to tell your father."

He lowered her into the deep luxurious settee.

He was so strong and sensual, she knew he could overpower her with little or no provocation. Then suddenly, he was mocking her naivety.

"Christ Almighty! What possessed you to think the worst of me? I'm not in the habit of paying for favours, they fall into my lap with little or no incitement on my part. As for you, young lady, when we get to the stage of making love, you'll want it as much as I do".

He held her securely to him for a short while then drew her to her feet. He followed her gaze to the floor where the notes were still scattered and said, "The money is for the clothes you will have to buy, treat it as expenses due to you. I hadn't time to arrange a credit account for you".

"I have clothes with me", she protested indignantly.

"I know you have and very nice indeed I must say, but you haven't worked yet so have never been able to buy sophisticated clothes suitable for business and maybe Paris".

She felt awkward about taking the money and hoped there would be a lot left over so that she could reimburse him with a considerable sum.

Mary was exhausted as she settled down into the comfortable bed. She relived the brief breathtaking moment that Ron had held her close to him and wished he had kissed her. She closed her eyes and with an intake of breath ran her fingers sensually over her firm heaving breasts while fantasising about making erotic passionate love with him. She turned over quickly and while trying to put the indecent thoughts out of her mind, had a vision of Shaun with his head stuck out of the car window. She smiled sleepily and whispered, "Thank you Shaun for being so endearing and including my paintings in your exhibition".

Chapter Five

Ron was worried about Kevin in the morning, as he had told him he wasn't up to the pace of the tough negotiating meetings, so if he didn't mind, he would give it a by.

"It's not like him, Mary, he usually likes to be in the thick of things, I'm worried he is worse than he is saying. I might have to forgo the French trip".

"Don't be a headcase" said Kevin from the doorway, "I'm not stupid, if I feel an attack coming on, I'll ring for the doctor".

"But you didn't last time, if it hadn't been for the cleaning woman coming in you might have died", Ron reminded him.

The chauffeur arrived for Mary and she looked anxiously towards Kevin, "What about a visit to the doctor this morning,Kevin?".

"Oh, off with you, I'm as right as rain and I don't want you fussing over me as well", said Kevin lightly as he accepted her kiss on his cheek as she passed by.

The chauffeur, who told her to call him Todd, took her to the selected shop previously arranged by Ron. When she got inside the shop manageress was obviously waiting for her and helped her choose the most suitable clothes for the occasions, she then left a friendly assistant to look after her. Mary was medium to tall with a perfect figure. The assistant said, "When we are through with you, young lady, you will look like as if you have stepped out of a fashion magazine".

After visiting a few other shops, and loaded down with three outfits, shoes, handbags and jewellery Todd dropped her back at the flat at exactly 11.15am.

They were first to arrive at the Hilton and waited in the foyer. Ron had time to give Mary an outline of the meeting. The property he wished to buy was the Château De Montville which was 40 kilometres north of Paris, near the town of Chantilly, the well known horse racing centre. If he was successful in securing it he intended converting it into luxury apartments. After much research into changing trends among people in that area seeking housing, particularly business executives and young couples, it was widely found that renting in the residential sector was on the increase. Even after extensive renovations, Ron was confident he would make a lot of money.

He stopped talking business and looked at her admiringly and said, "You look a million dollars".

"I should too with the fortune I spent on clothes today", retaliated Mary with all the confidence that being well dressed can give.

She was wearing a green and navy linen long jacket with diamante buttons and matching green linen skirt from Tomasz Starzewski. Her shoulder bag was green and matching shoes that were so comfortable they felt like a dream.

Monsieur Pierre arrived soon afterwards and made a beeline straight for them. He was a man in his mid-fifties or thereabouts, immaculately dressed in a fawn suit and striped shirt. Mary knew she had a difficult task ahead as she made the introductions. They made their way to the restaurant and were shown to their table. As they sat down, André, as he had asked them to call him, congratulated Mary on her choice of suit and told her she was extremely beautiful.

Mary blushed and said, "Merci, Monsieur".

"Je vous en prie Mademoiselle", bowed André.

"What was all that about?", Ron wanted to know.

"He was complimenting me on my exquisite taste in clothing", replied Mary.

"I'd better make sure I don't leave him alone with you. You have to watch these French men, they are over sexed and have a few mistresses in tow as well as a wife", warned Ron crisply.

Mary glanced at André who was scanning the menu and said to Ron in a hushed voice, "Be careful what you say as some French people find it a great honour to be spoken to in their native language therefore they hide the fact that they can speak some English".

She wondered if, when she looked in André's direction,

he had understood what she had said as she thought she saw a muscle twitch on his jaw as if he was suppressing a smile.

Anyway it seemed to do the trick with Ron as he spoke more cautiously during the meeting.

"The Château De Montville has certainly potential but it will need extensive work done on it to make it sound", being careful not to mention his father's name Ron went on, "A very professional body from England has checked it out and found that the foundations need to be reinforced, which is quite an expensive job, not to mention the reinforcement of interior stud walls".

"The asking price for the chateau remains at £675,000. Three estate agents valuations came within a hair's breadth of each other's quotes. They all agreed unanimously that the château occupied one of the finest positions in all of France", said André stubbornly.

They wrangled on for some considerable time each trying to outwit the other and Mary found this hard going, slipping in and out of languages continually and at the same time taking notes of the important issues. She felt she couldn't even excuse herself as they would have to sit like stooges.

André eventually excused himself, declining coffee, when they were shown to a luxurious lounge. He bowed to Mary and said he would return in a few minutes.

"I agree that it is a prime situation but the valuation

reflects that and he has given very few good reasons why he considers that the asking price is already a bargain so I won't complete a deal until he drops his price by a minimum of £35,000", said Ron when André was well out of earshot.

Mary said, "In my humble opinion, for what it's worth, I suggest you concentrate on the advantages your offer brings him, after all the man is in no financial position to take on the renovations that are needed to make it viable".

Ron gave André ample time to settle himself into the seat before putting forward his case. "We both know that you are in no financial situation to convert the château into flats and also buyers of this type of property are few and far between. As inflation falls and prices remain static people are once again looking at renting. If property purchase is not going to give people the investment they had hoped for they will look at the relative cost of rent and mortgage and will very often take the short term view".

André tried unsuccessfully to outwit him but eventually said, "I have no intention of dropping the price more than...", he hesitated to convert francs to pounds then said, "£30,000".

"I have no intention of buying from you for a penny more than £630.000."

"£640,000 and we will shake on it", said André hopefully.

"£630,000 or no deal", retorted Ron.

André Pierre turned to Mary after he and Ron had shook hands on the deal and said he was very happy to show them around the Chateau De Montville tomorrow at 5.00pm.

Mary repeated this request to Ron. Anticipating an invitation, she had written out a short phrase for Ron to use.

"Chic alors! Avec plaisir, merci André', said Ron making a good effort and taking André by surprise.

In faultless English André replied with a beam from ear to ear, "I look forward to meeting you both. Good afternoon". He shook hands and walked off.

"What a cheek", said Ron. "He knew that, although most of the time you conversed in perfect French, there were the odd occasions when you were struggling and he didn't offer any help".

"That is their way", laughed Mary and added, "Are you happy with your acquisition?".

"Yes, very! Thanks to your rational thinking".

"Oh, I played a very small part, but you were marvellous", smiled Mary.

Todd was waiting to take Ron and Mary back to the flat, but Ron asked to be dropped off at the office as he had to get his secretary to arrange accommodation and currency for the French trip, so Mary was left back at the flat alone.

Kevin let her in and was overjoyed to hear that Ron had secured the Château De Montville.

As they sat talking over a glass of wine, Mary wondered if she dare mention Katie, but decided against it as it would be better to speak to Katie first. Then suddenly out of the blue Kevin said to her, "Katie was the loveliest, kindest person one would ever have hoped to meet and one of the greatest regrets I have in this life was that I wasn't forceful enough with her. I should have made her marry me".

"Do you still love her?", Mary asked.

"I'll love that woman till they take me away in a coffin".

"Well, why don't you be forceful now and get together again", said Mary hopefully.

Kevin threw his head back and laughed, "Oh Mary you don't know Katie at all. It was as much as she could bear, the other night, to speak to me on the phone and leave that message for you. I'm afraid she hates the ground I walk upon, it's as bad as that".

"What happened between you, that turned her against you so much?", Mary asked.

"Oh, something and nothing, but as I said, she is a stubborn woman. She fell out with your mother roughly around the same time and it was the height of nonsense that those two girls never got together again. They were inseparable from birth and suddenly a little incident slashed them apart, I never understood it and I won't till my dying day".

Ron overheard Kevin's last sentence as he appeared and Kevin decided to tell him about Katie ditching him on the eve of their wedding. "It's in the past now but I suppose it is a matter of courtesy to let you know, also so that you can avoid making arrangements that involve Katie and myself meeting again".

"You should have warned me the day I told you she was coming to dinner, we could have saved Katie a lot of embarrassment", said Ron.

"I was a silly old fool, I hoped she would have let bygones be bygones at least, but I was wrong and I am sorry now", replied Kevin listlessly.

Kevin decided to change the morbid subject and informed them that he definitely had made up his mind to give France a miss and that there would be plenty of time for visiting when the contract was exchanged.

André Pierre proved to be a most generous host, he welcomed them warmly to the Château De Montville. He informed them that he had laid on a banquet in their honour, to commence in the early evening after he had shown them round the château.

The château stood at the end of a long drive, with pillared

portico bay windows and attractive arched dormers in the slate roof. It enjoyed a fantastic secluded setting overlooking lakes on both sides. The grounds had been kept in very good order, mostly lawns and well placed shrubs and large magnificent colourful rhododendrons. The same could not be said of the interior of the château. The Gallery room, obviously once elegant and reflecting French taste, showed signs of chipped plaster panels and columns, patched stained glass windows and dry rot in the window ledges.

The château contained ten large bedrooms with high ceilings. For modern apartments, Ron pointed out, they would have to be dropped and each bedroom would have to include an en suite bathroom. He assured André that the rest of the house would retain its original character.

The one room in the château which was kept in splendid condition was the room where the banquet was to be held, The Great Dining Room. It was a magnificent room with a high ornate ceiling and a wealth of fine paintings, mostly in oil, and an area kept for watercolours of French villages. The large painting above the fireplace was the magnificent "Les Perruches", by Jean Dupas. The walls were decorated in brocade wall covering in violet and grey. The centrepiece of the room was a grand and diverse clock built in marble, free standing roughly three meters high, probably designed to remind people of time passing but also of their own mortality. André laughed as he saw Mary checking her watch and said, "We have observed that most people's first reaction on encountering the clock is to look at their watches for reassurance.

"I shall be very sad to give up the ownership of the château. I knew the buyer would very likely be a business man and very possibly a foreigner. I am indeed happy to transfer it into your capable hands, Ron", said André.

André spoke in reasonably good English to Ron but when speaking to Mary he broke into French and Mary felt it was her duty to reply in French, which pleased André very much.

Ron and Mary excused themselves to return to the hotel which was only a short drive away in order to dress for the evening banquet.

Mary called, "Just a minute", in reply to Ron's tap on the bedroom door. She had been allocated a room one floor above Ron's. On opening the door she was stunned by his stylish appearance in evening wear. They both spoke simultaneously, she with, "You look terrific!", and he saying, "My, you are bewitching!", and again with a simultaneous, "Thank you". They both laughed as they walked cheerfully down the corridor towards the lift.

Mary had worn the white silk cloche sleeveless petal skirted shift dress with belt and bolero jacket which she had bought in London on her shopping spree. The silver fish scale necklace and matching earrings and bangle set it off to perfection.

André had arranged a party of about fifty people including his very attractive, well preserved wife, Marie-Noelle and two daughters, fifteen year old Jacqueline and Gabrielle, nineteen. He and his family received them in the spacious hall and there were introductions all round. Jacqueline was obviously a tom-boy and didn't feel comfortable in her evening dress and Gabrielle kept reminding her to straighten up her shoulders and hold up her head. Jacqueline obviously hadn't been paying attention during introductions as she enquired of Ron, in impeccable English, "Are you and your wife going to take up residence in the Château De Montville during the refurbishing?".

Marie-Noelle, her mother butted in, "Ron is the new owner of the Château and Mary is his secretary, I do wish you would pay attention".

Mary blushed in her dilemma and Gabrielle then said, "Now look what you have done, you have embarrassed Mary".

The tittle-tattle went on with Jacqueline defending herself by saying that Ron and Mary looked married and in love and Marie-Noelle apologising for her.

They entered the great dining room where the banquet table had a centrepiece of cleverly decorated fruits of guava, lychee star fruit, mango and banana with a mixture of nuts piled high.

They had never experienced such gourmet cuisine delights as they sat through the seven courses. Mary began to feel tipsy as each course was accompanied by a different wine. Family friends toasted André; André toasted Ron; Ron toasted André and so it went on, everyone thoroughly enjoying themselves. Ron had anticipated the wine so had arranged a chauffeur driven car to take them back to the hotel.

The guests gradually left the dining room and assembled in the Pink Drawing Room, where there were even more drinks on offer. Ron was quick to notice Mary's flushed appearance and she had acquired an extroverted attitude which he knew to be out of character for her so he made the necessary arrangements with André for their brief meeting the following morning and shook hands all round. The Pierre family saw them to the car and shrieked well wishes after them as they drove off.

On the short drive to the hotel, Mary settled her head on Ron's shoulder and he immediately put his arm around her and drew her to him. She was almost asleep as she felt his lips seek hers and responded hungrily.

Inhibitions disregarded she whispered against his lips, "Oh Ron, I want you so very much".

Ron lifted her bodily out of the car when they arrived at the hotel and put her onto her feet on the pavement. With his help she found her footing and walked to the door of her bedroom. She clung to him making no effort to look for her key so he fumbled in her bag until he found it and opened the door, helped her in then closed the door behind them.

Mary woke up feeling nauseated in the morning and swung her legs out of the bed unto the floor. She was stark naked and put her hand up to her head and thumped it trying to remember why she didn't put on her nightdress the previous night when suddenly the memory of it all flooded back to her. The last thing she could remember was clinging to Ron seductively while he undid her necklace and bangle. Then he started to undress her; firstly taking off her bolero then undoing her belt. After that - nothing - it was a blank. She made her way to the bathroom and was sick.

There was a knock on the door, so she pulled on her robe and opened it. It was a young maid with her breakfast on a trolley but enquired if she would prefer to have it in the dining room. Mary said, "Je veux consommer sur place, s'il vous plaît".

The maid pushed the trolley into the room and pointed at an envelope then departed.

Mary poured the coffee and didn't feel much like anything else, then she opened the envelope and read Ron's note.

Mary
I have left you to have a quiet morning recuperating after last night's bender. My meeting with André should be through by 12 noon. I will meet you in the hotel foyer at 1.00pm.
Ron

She looked at herself in the mirror, she never looked more ghastly, pale with large black eyes. My God what have I done and what will Ron think of me, she thought, as she remembered that the only thing that mattered to her last night was Ron; wanting him body and soul exclusively.

Her robe fell open and, looking now at her naked body, she felt thoroughly ashamed. She had been bashful of showing her body to anyone, even in the changing rooms at school she had kept herself covered so that the other girls could not see her, yet last night Ron had taken off her clothes and it never occurred for her to stop him. But what happened after he had stripped her naked? He will simply think that I am a slut and come to think of it, I felt like a slut. She had lusted after him with an intensity never known to her before and she felt disgusted and ashamed of herself.

Her head was throbbing so she poured herself a glass of water and dropped two soluble aspirin into the glass and without taking time for them to dissolve, guzzled it down recklessly, chewing the remains.

After showering she dressed carefully, choosing a cool casual chic suit in a red cotton crinkle textured fabric and a white short sleeved cotton embossed shirt.

She had some time to spare so walked through the splendid gardens at the rear of the hotel. It was pleasant and peaceful but her thoughts were in turmoil and she wished she was back home with Aunt Katie.

"How are you this fine afternoon?", Ron's words broke into her thoughts and she turned around to face him. He was standing before her smiling and looking handsome in a pale linen suit and green polo shirt with jacquard trim on the collar and placket.

She flushed but tried to regain her cool, then answered,

"Oh a bit of a headache, probably caused by the caviar which I certainly was not used to, but otherwise surviving".

"I'm sorry, it was my fault; I should have known someone like you wouldn't have had the experience to deal with all of that last night".

"All of what?" she asked hesitantly, feeling the dreadful flush creeping over her face again.

"All that immense amount of drink they thrust on us", he replied, "Why, what else were you thinking of ?".

"Whatever happened after we got back, I take full responsibility for it, something came over me and I want you to know it was completely out of character for me to throw myself at a man" she wailed with her eyes lowered.

"You don't need to apologise for yourself last night", Ron said tenderly taking her hand in his and steered her down the path, "and don't worry, your virginity is still intact".

That really did make her cry and he put his arms around her drawing her to him, "As I have said to you before, if and when I make love to you it will be with your full approval".

"You would have had that last night", Mary whispered into his neck.

"No, I had not, you were sozzled last night, you didn't know what you wanted and anyway you passed out on me", he said humorously.

"Why did you leave me naked in bed?".

"I wasn't exactly sober myself you know, I knew how to take your clothes off but I didn't feel capable of dressing you again", he smiled.

She stood on tip toe and planting a kiss on his cheek said, "Thank you, Ron".

He put both his hands on her shoulders, then slowly ran them down her short sleeves until they reached her soft bare arms. He looked into her eyes and thought of all the passion she wished to unleash on him the previous night and was unable to resist drawing her into his arms. He could feel her desire intensify again as she pressed her firm breasts against him and her arms reached up to cross each other tightly around his neck.

He cherished the glorious feeling for a few minutes before gradually releasing her and her arms fell from round his neck. His features took on a serious look, "Mary, I can't take our relationship any further for the time being".

Mary was taken aback, felt as if she had been struck, but replied simply, "Fine".

"Well", said Ron proudly changing the subject, "I am now officially the new owner of the Château De Montville, I wrote André Pierre his cheque this morning and you would never guess what he said to me on leaving".

"No, I would never guess", said Mary, as she linked arms with him on the way back into the hotel.

"The rude devil said, 'Ron, with reference to what you said about Frenchmen the other evening in London, I will have you know that when I turn over in bed, I like to remember who I am with and I don't ever have to get up at dawn and get out'".

Mary threw back her head and laughed.

Todd was waiting for them at the airport and drove them straight to Ron's flat.

"Father", called Ron like a child arriving back from school and Kevin appeared, looking extremely well and greeted them warmly. It seemed to come naturally for Mary to kiss Kevin but was disappointed when he said he would be off in a few hours.

Ron went through his post and Mary caught him off guard with a worried look on his face, but when he met her glance it disappeared as if she had imagined it and he smiled at her as she listened to an assortment of things Kevin had got up to while they were away.

"I wouldn't like to live in London but I sure as hell enjoy a break in it", Kevin said. "Alas, all good things have to come to an end".

"When will I see you again, Kevin?", Mary asked as Todd arrived to take him to the airport to get a flight to Leeds.

"Don't you fret, my girl, I intend going back to the Manor the week end after next so I'll see you then. I have no intention of being done out of a game of golf just because Ron had a business trip".

"That's fine by me, I'll have a round with you", said Ron as he shook his father's hand.

"I don't mind if Katie knows that I will be there, but assure her I won't come within her range", said Kevin seriously, as he bid Mary goodbye.

Mary rang Katie to let her know that she would be arriving back the next day and Katie told her there were a lot of replies from the agencies she had applied to but added, "I hope you will be in no hurry getting a job as I really love having you here and I have missed you these last few days".

"I've missed you too, Aunt Katie", said Mary as she rang off.

"Shall we visit the restaurant you so enjoyed a few nights ago", enquired Ron when he finally shut his briefcase.

"Actually, I don't feel like going out tonight, Ron, thank you, we had such a big lunch, I will just have whatever Kevin has left in the fridge".

"Same goes for me", said Ron, "You stay right there, I will make us something light".

Ron brought in a tray of carved turkey and ham, a selection of M & S salads and a bottle of chilled white wine and two glasses.

When they had finished their meal, Ron came and sat next to her on the plush suite putting his arm around her. While tracing her soft cheek with his free hand he asked, "We have no chaperon tonight, are you going to feel safe with me?".

Mary quickly drew in her breath and felt the longing for him as his touch sent strange messages through her body. She said nothing but turned into his arms and sought his mouth with hers. She gave and received kiss for kiss hungrily and instinctively pressed her body against him seductively while he moved his lips across her cheek then slowly down into her throat where she could feel his quickened hot breath as he disengaged her blouse running his hands sensually over her slender bra-less back then slowly, provocatively round to cup her soft curved breast. Then he took one nipple between his lips and teased it with his tongue, the sweet sensation in her nerve-cells sent a wild uncontrollable jangle through her body.

What now? Should she start unfastening the buttons on his shirt? With an overwhelming urge to press her breast against his hard chest, she timidly and cautiously ran her fingers down the front of his shirt and indelicately unfastened one button.

Almost as if he had imposed a rigid self control on himself, he backed off teasingly, pulling her up and planting one more kiss on her forehead saying, "Off to bed, you gorgeous seductress, this could get out of hand. Good night! See you in the morning".

Mary suddenly felt exiguous and although she knew a flush was developing on her face she became brave and said, "If this is a game, the rules don't seem very fair. I know I'm a complete novice at it but in my view it looks like the man has the right to fondle or do whatever he likes with the woman's breast, but then when it's her turn to play, the game is suddenly over and he's won".

He threw back his head and laughed. "I'll answer that by quoting Shaw, 'The golden rule is that there are no golden rules'. I let you win, Mary. I reckon I lost that game, you see I didn't score at all. Aren't you lucky you were playing with me tonight and not McGready. He may not have let you win".

Her face was now bright red as she smoothed her dishevelled clothes and left him.

With the sound of his laughter still echoing in her ears she leaned her back against the bedroom door and pressed her eyelids hard together to keep in the tears. She was annoyed with herself for still longing for the man who had hurtfully mocked her inexperience. As she splashed her face with cold water in her en suite bathroom she could overhear him talking on the phone. "I'm sorry, Corrina, I received your note in the post but there was no way I could make it tonight, I got landed with my niece. I thought my father was going to be here to see to her but he left".

There was a pause then he said, "No I couldn't possibly leave her in London alone on her last night, it just wouldn't have done. I'll see you tomorrow night. Take care my love. Bye till then".

She heard the click of the phone and tip toed out of the bathroom feeling humiliated. 'Oh, mother, you tried to protect me from men but you didn't warn me about how much one can be shattered by them'.

In the morning Ron thumped on her bedroom door and asked if he could come in, opening the door as he spoke. She swung out of bed grabbing her wrap to cover herself and as she fumbled with the knot he said, "Why all this modesty, I've seen you in less than your nightdress".

"Not with my approval you didn't", she threw the words at him sourly.

"It didn't seem that way to me", he said sternly.

"You told me yourself that I wasn't in any fit state that night to make rational decisions", she retorted.

"Ah well, its a woman's prerogative for her to change her mind, I was certainly getting different vibrations last night and if it hadn't been for my sense of control you might not have been so pure and white this morning, 'holier than thou' young madam".

She knew he was right on one count but didn't believe him about his sense of control, he had simply amused himself kissing and fondling her but hadn't really wanted her, she had been a distraction for a while, what he really wanted was to have been with his Corrina. She felt the jealousy mount in her as she thought of him and Corrina together, no restraint necessary.

"What are you doing in my bedroom anyway", Mary asked angrily.

"I'm afraid I can't take you to the airport as Karen has included me in the early meeting, so Todd will call for you at 10.O'clock. I'll have to be off now, I've left a cheque to cover the days you worked for me".

"I don't need to be paid, the clothes cost a fortune, or do you want them back?", she added insolently.

"Sorry, they wouldn't fit me", he said as he ran down the stairs.

She felt like calling after him, 'Would they fit Corrina?' but kept her lips buttoned.

She was quiet as she sat in the car beside Todd and he wondered what had happened between them. They were so happy yesterday. I suppose she has found out about Corrina, he thought and wished Ron had met Mary first, she was such a delight to be with. The other one was a looker though, no doubt about it!

"Would you like me to stay with you till your flight is called?", asked Todd.

"No thank you, I'll be fine".

"Don't forget, Jack will be there at Aldergrove to meet you, watch out for him".

As they bid each other goodbye, he wished he could wipe the dismal look from her face.

Mary opened her handbag and looked at the cheque again. It was for an enormous amount. It was almost as much money as mother had earned in a month. For the first time in her life she realised that love was all. No amount of money or acquisitions could make up for it. All she wanted in the world was Ron's love and being new to this game felt depressed that the person one fell in love with didn't necessarily have to reciprocate that love. It was possible that he felt similar loving feelings for Corrina and if that was the case, the agonies ahead, in the name of love, would be immense.

She felt thoroughly dejected most of the flight and refused the refreshment on offer by the hostess. Suddenly she had a thought - All's fair in love and war! Yes, that's what I'll do, I'll fight for him, I'm going to fight that woman, Corrina, tooth and nail.

Uplifted by her new-found determination, and she was a woman of determination, she watched from the cabin window as the plane made it's decent.

Chapter Six

Ron drove slowly through the traffic on his way to Corrina's home in Chelmsford. His thoughts went back to the time they met. She was an older sister of Karen, his secretary, he had met her on the last day of the 'Space Age Technology' conference in Chelmsford. "My sister is giving a talk on Computing Technology and I have told her you will be there so she is going to look out for you afterwards". Ron could have done without waiting for that part of the conference but dutifully decided to make an effort to hear her sister's talk and maybe speak with her afterwards.

It was a very hot day and the organisers decided to hold the last few hours of the conference in the delightful gardens of the hotel.

Corrina turned out to be a stunning beauty, she had mid-length velvet black hair with a fine feathered fringe framing her heart shaped face, a shapely figure and brains thrown in for good measure.

She had the delegates in the conference bowled over straight away. "Let's break with tradition on this sweltering day and take off your jackets and ties and ladies discard whatever you wish". She went on to show off her tiny lap top computer and to explain that ten years ago, the technology this little thing does, would have weighed a ton. "Somewhere up there is the Space Shuttle, Endeavour, weighing a whacking great four tons here on earth, in space the weightless object could be manoeuvred by three men. However, the giant satellite contains within it enough computing power that would have taken up several satellites a few years ago. Here I am in the garden with my miniaturised technology and up in space above me a team of extremely brave astronauts is fiddling with its own version of compressed equipment, if you get my drift!"

Ron and everyone else were intrigued by her talk which went on and on without boring the pants off everyone.

She concluded, "Clearly, data compression is going to become an important feature of business computers. As we generate more data we will need more storage space. The answer is either to buy extra disks and storage devices, or to reduce the size of the files themselves. Data compression programs are much cheaper than buying extra disks, so they are doubly economical, saving space and money.

"However, you could save space, just lie in the garden in the sun and soon you will drift away, snoozing to your heart's content in the land of nod and not generating any extra data to take up more space".

She walked straight up to Ron when she was through, saying, "I am Corrina, Karen's sister, I was present when you were giving your talk on 'Computer-based technology to cope with the upsurge in demands for rented properties'.

Ron shook her outstretched hand and congratulated her on her talk. She just shrugged and said modestly, "It's my work, I should be able to talk about it and hopefully sell a few computers at the same time".

She told Ron there was a quiet bar where they could have a chat within walking distance. They got on well from the start and to Karen's delight, arranged to meet again.

He thought of her now; she was amusing, intelligent, good company and he liked her enormously. They had drifted into a relationship but everything had moved too fast for him and since he had met Mary, he knew it was not as a lover he needed her. He could never want her as much as he had wanted Mary last night and he was going to have to break loose, but gently.

She opened the door to him and kissed him lightly in greeting, "Well, thank goodness that niece of yours has gone, perhaps now I can have the love of my life back again".

Their friendship had gradually developed, through habit, rather than desire, into courtship. She was the more assertive of the two where the relationship was concerned and had recently hinted about getting engaged and Ron knew he had been drifting along until the inevitable happened. If he had not met Mary he knew he would very probably have been married within a year.

She had an abundance of energy and never seemed to get the balance right between her working, social and leisure time. Almost every time he came to see her he had to endure an up to date account of the latest computing technology.

After a few hours in her company, where she demonstrated how one could turn their PC into a print shop by using new graphic enlargements to give high-tech printing at a realistic cost, Ron made his excuses saying he had an exhausting day and had an early start next morning.

"But darling", she protested, "We haven't had time for each other, I thought I would show you my new Desk Top Publishing Program first".

He hurriedly kissed her cheek as he answered, "I'm glad you did, it was very interesting, but I'll have to love you and leave you now. I'll call you in a day or so and we will do a show in London".

He would very soon break off their courtship, at the very least, set about sowing a seed in her mind. It would be awkward as she looked upon him as one of her possessions, akin to her computers.

Katie brought Mary's breakfast to bed as she suspected she had overslept. She sat on the chair beside the bed listening to Mary talking excitedly about the Château near Chantilly and the good time she had in London, and sensed that she avoided mentioning Kevin. "I think I should go to the agencies in London next week to be interviewed for one or two of those jobs that they wrote to me about. The one in the Kensington area seems tailor-made for me", went on Mary.

Katie spied the photograph of Mary and Ron lying on the

dressing table and couldn't avoid seeing the sparkle in Mary's eyes as she clung to his arm. She stood up wearily saying to Mary, "Don't be in any rush!"

"Aunt Katie", Mary said as Katie reached the door, "I know about you and Kevin, you don't need to hide it any more".

Katie never looked back as she said, "That's it then, I don't want it ever mentioned again".

She slowly walked downstairs knowing that it would have been best if the girl had never darkened her door.

Mary kept herself busy in the days that followed and also got round to ringing Shaun as she had promised. He was delighted to hear her voice, saying, "Mary, you got the message that you and I are jointly booked in Dunfanaghy on the 15th July. Please make a note of it in your diary". Then he went on to say, "I will drive over to Donegal one evening next week to give you guidance on getting the paintings ready for exhibiting".

She couldn't thank Shaun enough, knowing he had a very busy work schedule, but she did need his assistance in a few areas.

"Wednesday evening suits me, how does that fit in with you?", asked Shaun.

"Whenever suits you, suits me, I will tell Katie that you will be staying with us that night".

"Thank you, Mary", he said as he rang off, "I am looking forward to seeing you again".

On Wednesday evening, Mary laid out her paintings in readiness for Shaun's visit. She then went upstairs and changed out of her jeans into her pale blue cotton dress, combed her hair and dabbed on some lipstick and patiently waited for his arrival.

Katie and Shaun came in together chatting happily. Katie was saying, "Let's hope you can make our Mary as great an artist as yourself one day".

Mary was quick to observe his striking appearance as he came into view. Working clothes discarded in favour of an expensive designer rich wool suit in taupe and cream shirt and multi floral tie in pastel colours.

He came towards Mary with his hand outstretched and with a radiant smile, he said, "The talent is there, it is just a matter of time and a little bit of effort on her part before it all falls into her lap".

Mary was so delighted at seeing him that she ignored his hand and held out her arms to him. He gave her a friendly squeeze and said humorously, "Any more of that young lady and I'll not be responsible for my actions". He went on, "By the way I have arranged to meet a few friends later in the local pub, I hope you'll join us".

Katie put the kettle on while they made a start on the paintings. Shaun discarded his jacket and tie, then turned off the radio saying he never listened to music while he was working, "It occupies the same part of the brain as painting does. Now cricket, that's different", he added with a glint in his eye, "It acts like a sponge, wiping away stray thoughts".

Mary laughed at his logic. She tackled the paintings with complete enthusiasm under his guidance. He was a splendid teacher and by giving her a few tips the paintings were brought to life, but not without pains. She enjoyed his flair for words. "For this job", he said, "You have to have an infinite capacity for taking pains; pains are the embodiment of genius".

It was two hours before Shaun was fully satisfied that the paintings were ready for a signature and told her she had done him proud. "I am going to confiscate your paintings for the time being while I mount them personally in my workroom at home. They will be in safe hands and next time you set eyes on them will be at the exhibition".

Mary thoroughly enjoyed the friendly encounter in the local pub. As they entered a friendly voice called from the bar, "Ah Shaun, lovely to see you. What'll you have?" Shaun's answered in an equally lively manner, "A pint, Jerry, a pint of bitter".

"Now what will the lovely lady have, a lager?".

"Oh no, not a'tall, white wine for Mary, she's genteel!" he said as he put his arm round her shoulder and smiled.

Mary saw another side of Shaun, he was in his element among these people. The drinks had to be firmly on the table before the introductions took place. She liked his friends and they immediately accepted her as one of the throng. Amid hearty laughter the jokes flowed in a constant stream almost as fast as Murphy's Irish stout.

As the evening progressed, Shaun put his arm around her and spoke with his mouth against her ear, so that he could be heard above the singing of ballads, "Are you enjoying yourself ?".
She in turn spoke in his ear, "Haven't enjoyed myself more for a long time".

When they started singing 'At home in Donegal' Mary joined in only to realise that everyone had stopped and she was singing the last verse alone, accompanied by the guitarist, the words her mother sang so often -

The yarning then in the kitchen
As we gathered big and small
And my uppermost heart's desire
Is to be home in Donegal

Mary could hardly keep back the tears as she sang - for the first time in her life, she knew the meaning of the heart-breaking words.

They all clapped heartily when she stopped singing and wanted to know how she came to know the song and Mary explained about her mother coming from around these parts, which endeared her to them.

Katie had already retired when they arrived back and over a nightcap Shaun asked how she had got on in London and

France with Ron. He couldn't fail to notice how her eyes lit up when she spoke of him and knew that she had been smitten by the supercilious 'Lord of the Manor' type, who drove around in his Merc. He remembered the day Ron had nearly run him off the road as he was making his way to Katie's. They stopped and exchanged heated words, both blaming the other. Shaun had been driving along the track minding his own business, but then Ron claimed he had been doing likewise and was gratuitously offensive. Shaun, not wanting the egotistical upstart to have the last say, raised his fist to him as he watched him storm off.

Mary was an adorable person and Shaun had hoped to get closer to her in time. Being Irish to the core, he didn't believe in rushing things, but now he could have a rival in the form of that jumped-up unauthentic so called gentleman.

He got to his feet and said, "I'll have to bid you goodbye now as I have to be up with the lark, unfortunately I have an early start in the morning".

Mary was disappointed, but laughed as he said, "I'll have another one of those smackers now that you threw at me, landing God knows where", and drew her into his arms. His lips held hers gently, neither wanting to be the one to end it. They drew apart tenderly and wished each other goodnight.

Later Mary lay in bed staring into the shadows hoping that nothing would manifest itself that would come between the friendship she shared with Shaun. She couldn't bear to ever hurt him.

Mary was sitting by the fire reading when the door bell rang, she felt as weak as a kitten when confronted with Ron.

She reacted stupidly, saying, "Katie is out for the evening with her friend".

Ron pushed her inside and closed the door saying, "Good, I've come to see you". He pulled her unceremoniously to him and kissed her long and hard, while she reciprocated eagerly. Holding her away from him in an effort to summon some composure he said, "My God, you have taken over my life! In the middle of an important business meeting I find myself thinking of you. What have you done to me you slip of a lass?".

Mary leaned her head on his shoulder and thanked God she wasn't going to have to fight for him after all. Then it all came back. "But what about Corrina?", she asked hurriedly.

"I love you, Mary, but she is a little problem I have to sort out, I promise you I will. But how did you know about Corrina?".

"I overheard you talking to her on the phone the night we were on our own; it broke my heart".

"Damn! I forgot about that wafer thin wall, I'm sorry my darling, I would never, ever hurt you intentionally".

A horn sounded outside and Ron said, "My father is in the car, we met up at Luton Airport and caught the same flight. We are playing golf in the morning. I'll call for you at 2 O'clock, be ready to go out for the rest of the day. Do you love me sweetheart?".

"Yes, I love you with all my heart", Mary said kissing him goodbye.

When Katie returned, Mary told her that Ron had arrived for the weekend and he had invited her out the following afternoon. Katie didn't look that pleased and shrugged it off. Her attitude to Ron was unreasonable, thought Mary. Simply because he was related to Kevin, whom she didn't like, it didn't follow that all his relations should be spurned. She tried to say as much to her, but Katie just repudiated them both, mumbling, "Tarred with the same brush!".

Mary went off to bed but tossed and turned most of the night, torn between loving Ron and offending her aunt whom she had come to love like a mother.

Kevin and Ron made an early start towards the golf course that Kevin had been captain of many years ago. He hadn't played here for a very long time and was looking forward to it tremendously.

In days gone by, he had won a junior championship and got Ron interested from the early age of 15, as soon as he met up with him in fact. From then on he took Ron to as many of the championship golf matches as he possibly could. Kevin always played superb golf but Ron struggled to motivate himself and was dragged down by his putting nightmares. He improved as the years went by but had to fight for consistency.

Kevin, a keen club man, could easily have been a pro but declined in favour of his business.

They mixed banter with a conscious effort to enjoy the game but it was tricky, some greens were holding and some weren't. They hit the ball from tee to green pretty well all morning but there were not too many birdies flying about and they both just hung in there. Kevin was in the lead mostly from start to finish, he kept in total control of his game. He succeeded in breaking the pattern of the day with a birdie at the two hundred yard par-three tenth. He loved this course where he had been the winner on big occasions. All in all it was a close game and Ron seemingly set to come in two shots behind crashed with a double bogey six at the 17th. The line of approach seemed right, but it bounced off and finished up in a bunker in somebody's footprints. "I had a double bogey, and I did nothing wrong", he groaned.

They packed their clubs into the car and changed out of their golf shoes and went to have a beer at the bar which remained fundamentally unaltered from the old days.

After they had brought their drinks back to a table, Kevin stared towards the bar and deep in thought remembering the sight of Matt, a disheartened man with slouched shoulders as he threw back the spirits, while he himself had fooled around on the dance area. His eyes wandered from the bar to the dance floor and he had a visual impact of the beautiful girl clowning in an extroverted manner.

She was more precocious and vivacious on that evening than he had ever remembered her before. He could see her laughing face now and the outfit she was wearing, an off the shoulder dress of pink lace and her shapely breasts which he was to touch and kiss later, he could remember to the year, month and hour...

"Hi, a penny for them", Ron's voice broke into his thoughts.

"Ah, the place is full of ghosts, I couldn't help thinking of Matt, Mary's father, he died young you know".

They made their way back to the car stopping to read the names on the plaques of former captains where Kevin proudly pointed to his name. He smiled as he told Ron about the old days when they had to chase the cows off the fairway. The club had only fifty members with an annual subscription of a few guineas and playing was banned on Sundays.

They drove back to the Manor and Kevin assured Ron he was looking forward to a nice quiet day in the grounds, whenever he wasn't watching sport on the television of course. "Go off and enjoy yourself, you deserve some relaxation to offset the life you lead in the fast lane".

Katie answered the door to Ron and invited him in to wait for Mary. He made no conscious effort to hide his affections for Mary from Katie. As Mary came down the stairs their eyes met tenderly and his heart sang.

"Have a nice time", said Katie to them both.

Mary hoped Ron didn't notice Katie's aloofness as she was usually very affable. Her words, in normal circumstances, would have been accompanied with a smile.

As they drove off Ron said, "I have thought about going to Tory Island, I haven't been before, is that alright with you?"

Mary snuggled against him saying, "Anywhere in this world is alright as long as you're there".

Ron, giving her a sideways glance, noted how her happiness reflected radiance.

They took the ferry from Magheraroarty Pier across to Tory Island. The crossing from the mainland was known to locals as being very often rough, but they hit it lucky to-day and had a reasonably smooth crossing. Ron told Mary that he had read up on the Island and that it had a long history and had been inhabited since prehistoric times. They were very impressed by the village of West Town, the medieval round tower was built from pink Donegal granite and cemented with lime made from sea shells; although it was partially in ruins Ron told her that it had stood for 1000 years despite the buffeting from the fierce Atlantic gales.

They decided to split from the crowd of day trippers and went slightly off the beaten track and sat down on a very secluded and well kept grassed area to enjoy the appetising snack that Alison had prepared for them.

Ron suddenly thought of a write-up in the Telegraph that morning about McGready. He read that he had an exhibition running at the Academy's new Sackler Gallery and at the same time work on show at the Nigel Greenwood Gallery. He also played his part among the judges for the Royal Academy summer Exhibitions.

"Mary, how interested are you in this painter fellow?", Ron threw the question at her and caught her off guard. She swallowed a bite of her sandwich too quickly and almost choked herself. Ron hit her hard on the back till she stopped coughing.

"He has been my unpaid tutor and a good friend, coaching me on the paintings. That is all!" said Mary at last.

"What paintings are those?", he asked.

"I went out with him on four occasions and we painted some delightful scenery. Also, I am putting the painting of the Manor into the exhibition, plus a few others".

"What exhibition?", he asked, surprised.

"Oh, one held locally in Dunfanaghy on the 15th July".

"You mean you are trying to sell the painting you did of the Manor, without showing it to me first? ", he said harshly.

"You are very welcome to come along to the exhibition", said Mary gloomily.

She admitted her mistake straight away and apologised for not consulting with him before deciding to display it at the exhibition. "Shaun chose it to go forward to the exhibition and I simply didn't think to tell you".

"I'm not going to the exhibition, I don't like the fellow and I want to buy the Manor painting. Tell him to put a sold sign on it before displaying it".

"You haven't even seen it, you may not like it and you don't know how much he is going to ask for it!".

"I said put sold on it".

"Right, I'll tell him. Ron, please don't lets spoil this lovely day", she said.

Ron looked into her eyes, he could see the soft glow of love shining out of hers for him. Damn you, McGready, she's mine. Thank God!

He took her by the shoulders lowering her into the grass and kissed her time and time again, longingly; each kiss becoming more and more demanding. Suddenly things began to move too fast and before she had time to fathom his intention he undid the zip of her skirt just enough to reach in and lift the edge of her silk underwear and caress her body with gentle fingers; a deep groan of passion escaped his lips and the effect of it inflamed her. "I love you, Ron", she whispered opening her lips to savour his moist tongue as her slim fingers tunnelled through his hair. She was totally in his power and would stop at nothing.

"You are the most exhilarating thing that has ever happened to me in my entire life and I want you so much, my darling, but if you say that you will marry me soon, I'd like the first time to be in my four poster bed". Ron's words fell on her ears like serenading music, but she was too busy kissing him to answer.

Ron decided they would take the helicopter for the return journey as there were early signs of a storm.

On the drive home they sat contentedly listening to love songs on cassette. She used to think those people were mad that drove around unable to keep their hands off each other; now at last she could empathise with them as she snuggled closer to him.

He kissed her goodnight and made arrangements for her to visit the Manor the following day. "My father will have my life if I don't share you with him, I'd much prefer to have you all to myself".

He went round to her side of the car and as she stepped out he once again enclosed her in his arms saying, "Tell me how much you love me again?".

"More than anything in the world", she answered with stars in her eyes. They clung together both wishing they didn't have to part.

Mary went into the house feeling happier than she had ever felt in her life.

"Aunt Katie", she called, "There's going to be a storm!

We took the helicopter back from Tory Island".

She found Katie sitting at the kitchen table and Katie asked her to sit down.

She couldn't think what Katie wanted to tell her but thought it might be important by the look on her face so she pulled off her jacket and flung it over the chair inattentively and sat down opposite her.

"Is anything the matter, Aunt Katie?", she asked.

"No, but I have made up my mind that I will open your mother's letter", she said as she drew the envelope from her pocket.

Mary was glad and relieved, she had worried lately that Katie would destroy the letter unopened, without telling her.

Katie tore the letter open, and inside were two envelopes, one addressed to Katie and the other to Mary. She handed over Mary's envelope and asked her to open it first.

"Mother didn't have to do this, she could easily have given it to me herself or better still, discussed it with me", said Mary cautiously.

"She must have had her reasons, perhaps if I didn't read mine then maybe it would be best if you didn't read yours", said Katie with wisdom.

Mary held onto the letter unopened for some time, it was

eerie, knowing that her mother had been the last person to hold it. With some trepidation she tore open the letter and her mother's familiar hand writing appeared in front of her as she unfolded the pages.

She then smoothed the sheets on the table before starting to read.

My Dear Mary

I hope you look back on your life with me in happiness and feel no regrets. I tried my best not to smother you even though it was difficult as my love for you was tremendous.

Well here goes - Matt and I had been boy and girl friends from when I was fourteen and he was eighteen. He made no bones of his love for me and I loved him in return but not in the same deep fashion. We went everywhere together and had a happy courtship. He had a lovely personality and always full of fun. We got engaged just before our parents were killed and he was a great comfort to me during those dark days that followed their death, and indeed to Katie also.

One day I was having a cup of tea with his mother while I was waiting for Matt to return from work, she told me she had something to tell me and went on to say she hoped it would make no difference to me marrying Matt as she knew he was besotted with me. "Matt had an operation when he was ten and he doesn't know that he will never be able to father children. I had it confirmed from two doctors", she said unhappily. To be quite honest the significance of her statement hadn't hit me till later, I had never even thought of having children at that stage. So I had been able to set his mother's mind at rest by telling her it didn't make one iota of difference to me.

It was uncanny how Katie and I had the same response to people, and when Matt made up a foursome with a friend, Kevin, Katie took an instant liking to him, as I did. Katie and Kevin started courting and she said to me, "I'm so glad you like him, as I really have fallen for him". Kevin was 28, a little older than Matt, he was the architect for the building company where Matt worked as a surveyor and a victim of an early marriage. He was divorced from his wife after only living together for ten months. He had one son and made an effort to keep his marriage going, but it became impossible and one day Belinda just walked out and went to her mother taking the baby with her.

I had become besotted with Kevin. It was difficult to keep my feelings concealed and that was essential as Katie was madly in love with him and I knew it would hurt her deeply if she were to find out.

When Katie and Kevin got engaged, we decided on a very quiet double wedding with only Kevin and Matt's families as guests. We only had two cousins that we had lost touch with and didn't even bother to look them up.

About six weeks before the wedding the four of us arranged to go to a dinner dance at the Golf Club where Kevin was captain for the year. Unfortunately Katie couldn't make it due to a bad throat infection which raised her temperature. We had a lovely evening all round and I tried to make up to Kevin for Katie not being there by dancing time about with him and Matt. As I was dancing with Kevin he suddenly pulled away from me when he noticed that Matt was throwing one drink after another into him. When we got his length he was in a bad state and started to hit out at Kevin, his good friend, and cry like a baby which was completely out of character for him. I put my arms around him and led him to the car, where he collapsed in a drunken state.

We took him home first and on the way to our house Kevin pulled into a layby to discuss Matt with me. He worried about him and sensed it was the beginning of a serious drink problem. I told him Matt tried his best and very rarely got as bad as that, something must have triggered it off that night and I was confident after we were married he would be alright as I would have more time and love to devote to him. I remember shivering as I tried to convince Kevin, because deep down I wasn't so sure. Kevin put his arm around me to comfort me, but he got more than he bargained for. I categorically take full responsibility for what happened between us that night. I turned into his arms with an uncontrollable desire and said, "Kiss me Kevin, I want you so much". Kevin tried to hold me off, saying, "Now is this being fair to me Sue! Just because Matt isn't here to satisfy you for God's sake don't pick on me". I held unto Kevin in a sensuous manner until his bodily demands got the better of him. He touched the lever down the side of the seat and it immediately collapsed. I can't even remember us grappling with clothes as we gave in to our desire. I only knew I was at a fertile time of the month and I loved Kevin with an intensity never known to me before. I could hear Kevin whisper, "Sue, you have me mesmerised, you are so lovely".

That was the one and only time I enjoyed making love, but I'll never forget Kevin saying afterwards, "There is no excuse for what I have done. There has never been anyone since Belinda and God knows I wanted Katie so much but I was willing to wait. What in heavens name came over you Sue, surely you could have waited for Matt?". I knew it would have been unwise to have told Kevin that I loved him more than I could ever love Matt and that I wanted one memory to have for the rest of my life, so I had to let Kevin think the worst of me. If only Katie hadn't been my sister, who I loved above anyone else in the world, I would have fought tooth and nail for Kevin.

Our friendship was ruined after that, he made up ways of being with Katie on her own rather than make up a foursome.

Two days before our wedding, Katie found out I was pregnant. Those mornings that I had been sick suddenly aroused her suspicion and she was the only one I had told about Matt never being able to have children. She knew that on the night of the dance I had come home later than I should have, in a dishevelled and anguished state, she had put it down to Matt's drunken condition. "My God, it wasn't Kevin, was it?", she cried with a sudden realisation. Katie and I knew each other too well to be able to keep secrets and my blushing to the roots of my head didn't help. She called us both the worst names on the earth and said that she was finished with both of us for good.

Matt's mother visited us when you were just a year and a half old and held you up at arms length and said, "Would you believe it, those doctors were proved wrong then and Matt fathered a child after all". Matt was surprised that I hadn't told him and I led him to believe that I had completely forgotten all about it.

Now I have told you Mary, it's up to you if ever you want to find your father and tell him. Please tell Katie to try and forgive me and that I have loved her always.

Your loving mother.

After reading the letter Mary stood up wearily, she was in no doubt as to the magnitude of the contents as she handed it to Katie saying, "I think this letter was meant for both of us, Aunt Katie, I'll leave you to read it in peace".

Mary stepped outside and lowered herself into Katie's rocking chair, the trees were swaying in the wind. She was numbed to the core by the implication of the letter. Just as Katie must have felt destroyed all those years ago, she lowered her face into her hands in utter devastation. There could not have been a more inopportune time in her life to have read such debilitating news. She touched her lips; they were still stinging from their incestuous passion.

This is inconceivable, Mary thought, I have to pull the same stunt on Ron that Katie pulled on Kevin all those years ago and give him the cold-shoulder. I have no alternative, it is the one, solitary, road left to me.

She was distraught as she sat and rocked to and fro. In

her traumatised condition, she was unable to comprehend the situation further.

Katie read both letters, the one to her had been short and to the point.

Dear Katie

I am writing this letter to you for myself as much as for you, I don't know if I will ever send it to you.

I never told you that I loved Kevin equally as much as you loved him. The years never lessened the love I felt for him. After Matt died there was nothing to stop me going after him and telling him he was the father of my child but my loyalty to you remained constant.

We both deserved a better deal on this earth and I beg of you, even now after all these years, if you still love Kevin and if he is available, for God's sake go to him and make the most of what time there is left. I thank God I was blessed with his child and I saw him every day in her eyes. Please extend the hand of friendship to my lovely daughter, she is an innocent victim because she so wanted a family and never knew the lovely father and aunt she possessed. I'm sorry she wasn't given the chance as a child of seeing the minnows in the stream at Falcarragh or playing on the Donegal shore, but hopefully one day she will cherish the joy of painting Glendowan and Derryveagh.

Your ever loving sister.

Katie stumbled through the door and looked down at Mary's tear stained devastated pale face, which had by this time taken on an automated, unconscious look. She fell to her knees beside her and cried into her lap saying, "Oh Mary, I can't bear to see you suffer, there ought to be a law to compensate the afflicted. I realised Ron was your brother as soon as I met Kevin that night, but God forbid, I never dreamt then that you and he would fall in love".

Her words fell on deaf ears, Katie knew Mary was beyond comprehension. "I know now that my sister suffered, perhaps more than I did and it is very, very hard to forgive her, she ruined all our lives, including Matt's, she drove him to an early grave and never gave him credit for knowing all along what was going on.

"She ruined my life and Kevin's. I have been left childless. I could never have married such a weak willed man at that time knowing he lusted after my own sister and fathered her child. God knows he has missed out on life too by her deeds. Now she has succeeded in ruining her only daughter's life from the grave, not to mention Ron's".

Katie knew she could talk for ever about the havoc her sister had caused them all but she couldn't deny the fact that she would need to look upon it in a different perspective. Even a strong man should be allowed one moment of weakness. As she remained on her knees she prayed, a little verse she had known a long time:

Give me, Lord

The courage to change those things that can be changed
The patience to bear those things that can not be changed
And the wisdom to know the difference.

She raised her head and looked towards the sky, by now there was a howling gale. Helping the dazed girl to her feet, she muttered, "We could be in for the worst storm this area has ever seen; lucky you took the helicopter, you might have been shipwrecked".

Mary stirred, turned into her aunt's arms and wailed, "We were shipwrecked Katie! We were!".

Katie closed Mary's bedroom door behind her and made her way wearily down stairs to the kitchen. She sat down at the large old fashioned heavy oak table, characteristic of an Irish homestead. Old memories, which had lain dormant for years, were raked up tonight and were as clear as day. It was in this very kitchen that Katie told Sue to go. She had taken all the money they possessed in the world out of the dresser and laid it on this table together with the national newspaper, advertising for people with Matt's skills, saying, "I won't have you living anywhere near me, I want you to get out of here tonight and I never want to see your face again in Donegal".

Katie felt she was justified in asking Sue to go, after all she was the one that was victimised and was going to be left without a man to support her.

Sue hadn't wanted to go and made a gesture of protest. "If you are going to take that attitude then I don't want to speak to you again either for as long as I live, but I don't see why I should leave Donegal. Matt and I love it here and we are looking forward to living in the cottage in Dunfanaghy. I want my baby to grow up in Donegal, its rightful heritage. I want my child to drink in the beauty as we have done, to see the sun turn the rocks red at Bloody Foreland. I want the isthmus of Sheep Haven Bay to be stamped on my child's mind and for it to run and play on the beautiful Tranarossan sands and scurry over the rocks at Marble Hill. I want it to frequent Rosguill, Horn Head, MacSwiney's Gun at Trawmore and... " Sue would have gone on forever as there is no end to the beauty of the area, but she stopped when she saw Katie pulling on her coat.

"Where do you think you are going in the dead of night?", she looked aghast.

"I'm going to wake up Jock Watson to take me to the airport. I won't live in the same country as you".

Things moved very fast after that; without further opposition, Sue packed her belongings and within an hour had left to go to Matt's parent's house. She heard they left the area on the 2 O'clock bus the next day, neither one of them to set foot back in Donegal in their lifetime.

The child had been an innocent victim and Katie thought of her constantly through the years - she nearly got to see her - just that once. She travelled with the Lavery's, Matt's parents, on the exhausting journey to Birmingham for the funeral. She ignored Sue's poignant and wretched figure at the graveside and grieved personally for the man and boy whose happy disposition deteriorated rapidly from the moment he introduced his friend to Sue. Before Sue was led off by well wishers, she stopped briefly and glared at Katie with hatred in her eyes.

The cemetery was deserted and cold as Katie sat alone at Matt's graveside and after a lot of deliberation, made her way to Sue's house. The house was full of mourners offering respects, but she answered the knock on the door personally.

"I want to see the child! She is my niece and I have no hostility towards her".

Sue slammed the door in her face but not before saying, in a desolate voice, "And I have no hostility towards Donegal".

A guilty conscience needs no accuser. Amid emotional anguish and painful soul-searching Katie laid her head in her hands and for the first time since the night her sister closed that door behind her, she cried her heart out for her; she had left a catalogue of misery in her wake, but her only sin was to fall in love with the wrong man.

Chapter Seven

Even the simplest of tasks seemed mammoth to Mary next morning in the aftermath of the storm. Her actions depicted every petty frustration. Ricky, the dog sensed that she was upset, laying his head on her knee and whining. She gave him a spontaneous pat but then just as briskly pushed him off as she gathered all the recruitment newspapers together. She needed to get away, and fast, but knew it would be unfair to let Shaun down after he had done so much for her. It was a matter of courtesy to attend the exhibition that her paintings were appearing in, although Shaun, himself, had exhibitions appearing all over the country and couldn't possibly attend all of them.

One job looked promising, it was located in Paris. Now that Ron had secured the Château De Montville he would be employing the local contractors to do the reorganising, and his visits there from now on would be few and far between. She had to be sure their paths would never cross or bring them in contact with each other again.

Mary read the fateful letter over and over. Her mother's written confession hadn't decreased her love for her in any way, on the contrary, it had only served to make her seem more human. She had steered clear of men and avoided getting into relationships with them for the rest of her life, knowing full well the agonies that went with them. Unfortunately she didn't live long enough to protect me from them, she thought.

She must stop dwelling on the fact that a short while ago

she had wanted Ron more than anything in the world and had been willing to act the brazen hussy and would have stopped at nothing. Thanks to Ron for his high principles and sense of propriety she was still virtuous in body if not in mind.

"Mary", her aunt's voice drifted through her thoughts, "Ron has just pulled up at the door, do you want me to handle him?".
Katie was taking this whole episode badly, she looked as if she hadn't slept a wink all night.

"Yes, please", she called as she made her way upstairs and locked the bedroom door. There was no way she could summon the courage to face him.

"Hello Katie, can I see Mary please? I must speak with her, I owe her an explanation".

His face fell as Katie got straight to the point, "Mary doesn't want to see you, Ron!".

"What is this? Where is she?", he asked taken aback. "Mary doesn't want to see you", Katie repeated firmly.

Ron pushed her aside more roughly than he intended and stormed into the house. "Mary! Where are you?", he called, going through the downstairs rooms like a flash of lightening, then taking the stairs two at a time. He went into a few of the rooms then stopped outside the locked door and thumped on it.

"What is it, my darling?", he spoke quietly, trying to calm

himself although his breath was coming in short stops and starts. He waited patiently for her response, then he turned his back and leaned against the door, lifting his head high and closed his eyes. After a while he ran his back down the door and brought himself to a sitting position on the floor and lowered his head into his hands.

"I love you, Mary, I know you love me. Please open the door and I will explain everything" he pleaded dejectedly.

Katie looked at the pathetic figure from the foot of the stairs and her heart went out to him. Memories came flooding back of Kevin pleading with her to forgive him but she never gave in. Never in a million years will she forget that day. Kevin thought he was asking forgiveness for being unfaithful on one single occasion, but she couldn't tell him about the child and the deceitful thing Sue was doing to Matt. In retrospect and with Sue's confession in yesterday's letter, she should have forgiven Kevin. There had been no call for everyone to suffer. Sue's suffering should have been enough.

The tears ran unheedingly down her face and when she turned around to go, Kevin was there, standing quietly before her. She looked him straight in the eyes, they held the gaze until he stepped towards her and held out his arms. Without wavering she went into them.

"I can't bear to see you cry, never could", he said in a shaking voice as his own eyes filled with tears.

The door had been open and he had walked in just in time to observe Ron's pleading with Mary and saw him slump to the floor.

"Can't you do something, Katie, they love each other, don't let history repeat itself".

"I can't do a thing, Mary will never have anything to do with him again, as long as she lives", she snuffled into his jacket as he held her against him.

Ron spoke eventually in a tormented voice, "Look, I can explain everything. I didn't ask Corrina to come here, she just arrived on the doorstep". Then with raised voice he added, "What the hell could I do, I couldn't throw her out, I had to be polite. It's the God's honest truth! I swear to you on my mother's life, I didn't invite her here, please believe me".

Suddenly all hell broke loose; Kevin cried out in pain and fell right out of Katie's arms onto the floor with a terrible thud.

"Ron, Ron, come quickly, I think your father is dying", Katie screamed hysterically.

Ron jumped down the stairs and was at his side in a flash, loosening his tie, while Katie dialled for an ambulance.

Kevin looked terrible, he had gone blue and was gasping for breath. Then his breathing stopped.

Mary charged down shouting, "Get away from him", and immediately started mouth to mouth resuscitation.

She kept it up until the ambulance arrived, but to no avail. The experienced crew took over: It looked hopeless but eventually, after what seemed an age, they got him breathing again with the aid of oxygen. They carried him out on a stretcher. Ron followed them into the ambulance throwing one final sorrowful glance in Mary's direction.

Her heart went out to him but no words were exchanged.

The one remaining nurse that had been left to gather up the equipment turned to Mary and said, "He was a lucky man that you were here".

Mary retorted, "You lot saved him, I did nothing".
"You kept him alive long enough for us to save him, it was all down to you".

Katie and Mary both cried, this time with relief.

The phone rang and Katie answered it. It was Alison inquiring if they knew where Ron and Kevin were. Katie had to break the sad news.

Alison said, "Oh my God, that is ghastly news. I'll just wait until Ron gets in touch with me. Thank you, Katie. We will all keep in touch".

Alison put the phone down slowly, then went in search of John.

She found him pottering in the greenhouse and they both discussed quietly what was the best thing to do.

Alison had been the one to open the door to Corrina. Before her stood the most attractive woman she had ever seen. Her peaches and cream skin was velvet smooth framed by black shining hair. She looked a dream in a tight fitting bottle green suit.

"Thank goodness I have found this place at last, I never dreamt about it being out in the wilds. I hired a car at the airport but I should also have hired a driver as I got lost on quite a few occasions, and nearly everyone I asked directions of spoke in a Gaelic Irish accent and didn't understand me either".

"Ah yes, a lot of the locals do speak Gaelic around here, you were unlucky to have asked the wrong ones", laughed Alison.

Corrina then looked past Alison and shrieked, "Ron darling, I am so glad to see you. Surprise! Surprise!", and ran straight into his arms.

"My God, Corrina, why didn't you tell us you were coming?", he retorted unbelievably as he held her away from him.

He dutifully made the introductions, "Corrina, this is my housekeeper, Alison. Alison this is Corrina, sister of my secretary".

They shook hands and Corrina said, "I don't know why you keep harping back to my sister, after all I am closer to you now than Karen".

Ron ignored that and said, "Come and meet my father".

"Ah", said Kevin lightheartedly, "So this is the beautiful Corrina I have spoken to on the phone and whom Ron has kept hidden from me".

"Well I am hidden no longer, I am here for all of you to observe and hopefully approve of", she laughed.

Everyone, with the exception of Corrina, could sense that all was not well with Ron, he had acquired an obvious awkward stance and said, "I have something to attend to, I won't be long. Will you please show Corrina upstairs to the guest room, Alison , then we will all have a drink".

Kevin had followed in Ron's wake.

Now Alison had the responsibility of looking after the girl, who was pleasant enough but obviously had chosen an inopportune time to arrive.

Mary watched Katie pace the room time and time again before she said, "Katie, why don't you ring the hospital and find out how he is?".

"Strictly speaking, Mary, you have more right to enquire after Kevin than I, you are his daughter, even if you don't want to tell him, you are a blood relation".

"He must never know, Katie", she spoke furiously, "And Ron must never know, if they knew it would drive them apart. Kevin can only have one of us, it must be Ron".

The phone rang and Katie ran to answer it.

"Oh, thank God, Ron! Thank God!".

A pause then she said, "No! Thank you for ringing Ron. Goodbye and try not to worry".

As she put the phone down, she said, "Ron said that Kevin is in the Intensive Care ward and for the present, sleeping peacefully. He also asked if you were ready to speak to him. I said you were not".

"I must get away, Aunt Katie, I can't face him ever again", Mary sighed.

"Look here child, you can't avoid him for ever. This carry-on of hiding behind closed doors can't go on. You have just got to take a firm stance and face the facts. Tell him .... oh tell him whatever you like, but get it over with once and for all", said Katie impatiently.

Mary knew she was right, but it was a perplexing task as she loved him more than she ever thought possible to love a man. To stand there and insult him with a fabrication of lies was going to be more than she could endure. She had to succeed in making him despise her while all she wanted in this life was his love.

"I managed it, Mary, years ago, I never set eyes on Kevin for over twenty years, it was an unforgivable thing on my part and I know now I shouldn't have done it, but with you it is a vital necessity, you simply can't ever marry him!".

Mary put her fingers in her ears like a child, then wearily said in defeat, "Yes, yes of course you are right. I will get it over with at the very first opportunity".

Katie knew there was one more thing to clear with Mary before they retired to bed that night. She knew it was an inauspicious time for her to broach the subject, as Mary was inconsolable at having to finish with Ron, but she had to do it now as time was running out, indeed it could be too late already.

She ventured cautiously, "Mary, what would you think if I were to make it up with Kevin, that is if he will entertain it after all I have put him through?".

"I would be delighted, Katie", she said, "I love you both".

They hugged each other but they both knew that it was touch and go with Kevin and that there was a worrying time ahead.

In the morning Katie set about making arrangements. She rang Ron and asked him to pick her up on his way to the hospital, then likewise rang her friend Lucy and asked if she could spare a few days looking after things while she booked into a hotel near the hospital to be near Kevin. Lucy was delighted to help and said she was looking forward to it and told her to give Kevin her love.

Katie wisely knew that Mary couldn't take over as she had too much on her mind and anyway she had to make arrangements about her own life.

Mary was in the process of drafting an application for a job in Paris when the door bell rang.

She answered it only to be confronted with Corrina. She had never met the girl before but didn't need any guesses as to who she was.

"I am Corrina Bonnington, I hope you don't mind me calling".

Mary, although shocked, bravely held out her hand and they shook hands firmly. She couldn't fail to notice her slender hands and beautifully polished nails as she said, "How do you do, I am Mary Lavery".

"I know! You are Ron's niece!", she said.

"Not exactly", said Mary smiling, "But he adopted me to suit his book. Please come in. Have you heard how Kevin is this morning?. I didn't see Ron when he collected my Aunt Katie, so I have heard nothing today".

"I think they are preparing him for surgery, it doesn't look too good. I only saw him for a short time and I liked him very much", said Corrina.

Mary liked this girl, she was easy to talk to and if it hadn't been for Ron, she would have liked to make a friend of her. Corrina was in her element when she knew Mary was interested in knowing more about computing. "I know I am a computer freak and I have to be careful that I don't bore the ass off people who are not interested, but I have the latest thing in my car which you might be interested in having a look at".

Mary couldn't believe how well they got on and they had a pleasant few hours together.

"I'm glad I've met you, Mary, I was actually a teeny weeny bit jealous of you when you were in London, now I only wish we had all got together".

She went on to say, "Ron and I have talked about getting engaged, but he is a bit cautious and is taking his time".

"Well, when it happens, I hope you are both very happy". Mary was envious but felt that as she couldn't have him then hopefully Corrina would.

Ron arrived and Corrina fleetingly kissed him in greeting and said, "Oh, you saw my car at the door!"

He handed Mary a note from Katie, "She can explain all about my father better than I", he said. "You go ahead of me, Corrina, and tell them I won't be long, I want to discuss the Château with Mary for a bit".

Corrina told Mary she would call to say goodbye when she was leaving that night.

When she left, Ron and Mary stood facing each other. Just as the strains of the past hours was telling on her, the cumulative traumas was taking its toll on him and he looked mentally and physically drained. The silence was prolonged, neither of them willing to terminate it, but eventually it had to end.

Ron spoke, "I love you, Mary, and nothing in this world is ever going to change that, I promise you".

Mary could easily have reiterated the words and it was heart breaking not to, but she said firmly and steadily, "I'm sorry Ron, it has all been a dreadful mistake. It has nothing to do with Corrina, I have simply realised I don't love you, never could. I was mesmerised by your stature, you awakened my womanly senses and I was vulnerable to say the least. I'm sorry, Ron, it was all fantasy on my part, I have now come down to earth with a bang".

She felt like smut and lowered her eyes when she couldn't bear the forlorn look in his any longer.

"I can't believe what I am hearing. I don't believe it!", he said his fingers bruising her upper arms.

She composed herself again and looked him straight in the eye and said, "It's your word against mine, Ron", and then despicably she twisted the knife even further by adding, "I love Shaun".

She knew he was wounded with the worst possible weapon, but wasn't prepared for his retaliation. He tightened his grip on her arms even more then flung her backwards onto the settee, pinning her down beneath his body. His face was a mask of desire as he bruised her with his lips, forcing hers apart. He was as pale as the driven snow as he employed brute force tactics. She struggled and freed her lips from his frenzied lustful kiss. "For God's sake don't do this to me, I can't let you do this", she pleaded as she kicked out at him and with all the strength she could muster tried to push him away. She was no match against his powerful strength and two buttons flew off her blouse and her breasts spilled out as he manhandled her with a viciousness she had never encountered previously. She screamed! The frightful terror in her voice got to him; his violence vanquished and he murmured breathlessly, "Forgive me, my darling; I would have stopped, believe me, I know I would. I could never, ever hurt you. I guess the proverb was fitting 'a hungry man is an angry man'. I made a promise to you, I'll keep it. The day I make love to you, you will want it as much as I do and god knows that day will come, I'll never, ever, give up".

He kissed her tear stained face by way of apology for his contemptible actions and said gently, "I think it is McGready that has you mesmerised and you will come to your senses before long".

She couldn't send him away entertaining hope in his heart, so she sank a final blow, saying, "No Ron, accept it, it is definitely over; I could never, ever, want you!".

He left her lying there, a dishevelled, trembling wreck, punished for her only sin, her parentage.

Mary felt tired and dispirited as she told Lucy she was going to lie down with a dreadful headache and to apologise to Corrina for not seeing her, also to convey to her that she hoped they would meet again.

Chapter Eight

The last person Kevin saw before going into the operating theatre was Katie, she hadn't left him for a second since she arrived. He accepted her, without query, and their fingers intertwined momentarily as they wheeled him away. Their eyes held the gaze until they closed the door behind him. She went off to ring Ron to tell him not to come in for at least four hours and she herself was going back to the hotel to wait.

She knew by his depressed voice it was all over between him and Mary. She said, "Don't worry about your father, he is a fighter and he will make it".

"He will make it for you, Katie, I know he will and thank you".

The surgeon had spoken to Ron earlier and he had conveyed the dreadful news to Katie as they drove to the hospital that morning. In his case there was an 80% chance of dying during the operation and if he lived his quality of life wouldn't be good.

During the operation surgeons were to strip a vein from his leg, clean it and use it to make grafts to bypass the blockages. Kevin's blood would then be able to flow normally.

Katie sat for hours in the hotel room knowing she might not see Kevin alive again. When she couldn't bear it any more she went back to the hospital. After what seemed to be a lifetime the consultant announced that he had pulled through.

She couldn't see him of course, but the feeling of elation enveloped her and she ran to ring both Ron and Mary. Lucy took the message and told her about Mary's headache and she felt guilty when she knew Mary was so miserable and she so happy.

Normally they kept patients for twenty four hours in intensive care after the operation but Kevin was kept for four days as his pulse was so weak. He made good progress after that and in a fortnight Katie drove him home to her cottage. Alison wanted him to go to the Manor but Katie was adamant; her one aim was to concentrate on getting Kevin better. She was going to see him through this thing to the very end and had read up on diets and so on.

She fed him on a diet of vegetables, pulses and wholemeal flour and he was walking around the room unaided within a week, and in six weeks a quarter of a mile.

He astounded the doctors and they had to admit it was miraculous and retracted the statement that his quality of life wouldn't be good as he had positively got back to full health. He knew full well he couldn't have managed without Katie. She had been encouraging, loving and attentive. "It was the least I could do for the mess I made of your life", she told him.

They had achieved a companionable togetherness, full of basic warmth and affection. Now that he was back to full health, desires of old could not be quelled.

He looked at her with love in his eyes and said, "Am I an old fool to ask this, but will you marry me Katie McGrath?".

She was light-headed as she answered clearly, "Yes, and the sooner the better, I thought you were never going to ask, people round about will think I am a scarlet woman living in the same house as a man".

His love for her was overwhelming and he swept her up in his arms and swung her around, repeating, "Oh Katie! Katie! I never thought, I'd see this day".

"Mary is coming home tonight, I can't wait to tell her", said Katie with shining eyes.

Ron visited his father also but Katie took great pains to make sure their visits never overlapped.

Each time Mary came back she saw an improvement on Kevin, but could hardly believe it when she saw him on this occasion. He hurried out to the car to greet her and helped her in with her case. She kissed then both and on hearing the news, heartily congratulated them. Kevin said, "I have been trying to persuade Katie to come with me on a short holiday. I could be doing with it, but she needs it more".

"I think it is a marvellous idea, you should have a mid-week break this Tuesday coming", she said.

"Don't be silly, we wouldn't dream of going while you are here", Katie replied hastily.

"Actually, if I can persuade Shaun to come for a few days, we could look after the place for you".

"Well, that's you put in your place, Katie, we will arrange something tomorrow".

Kevin had taken a great liking to Shaun the weekend of the exhibition. He had arrived the previous afternoon to get the paintings organised and took possession of his old room as Kevin had been using the study downstairs where Katie had a bed installed for him.

Mary had started her new job at that time, as Secretary to Michel Guerrin, Director of a stockbroking company in Paris and was loving it. She flew back for the exhibition.

It had been a great success. Mary couldn't believe it when she saw her paintings exhibited. They looked so professional. Shaun had taken just as much care with her frames as he had done with his own and each framed painting had been mounted with museum top quality ivory board. She gaped, astonished, when she saw the massive price he had marked on them. She then told Shaun of Ron's request regarding the one of the Manor and he marked the price up even further. She told him it wasn't fair, but he only answered, "I don't want the cursed upstart of a man to have it, but if he has to have it, then let him pay dear for it".

Shaun's paintings were an astronomical price but in the

first hour they were marked sold. They were indeed masterpieces, she was proud to have been with him on the days they had been created. He had captured a rare beauty and she felt she was back again at the scene as the delicate hand painted colours retained the freshness and vibrancy of the day.

It proved to be extremely worthwhile for art lovers and collectors alike. The browsers, throughout the day found his paintings a joy, once seen, never to be forgotten.

Mary was delighted that her other two paintings were sold before closing time. As they left the hall, Shaun put his arm around her in a friendly manner and said, "Well, how are we going to celebrate with our well earned loot?".

"I'm keen to do anything you want to", she answered cheerfully.

"I know where there is traditional Irish dancing, I'll take you there. You are in for a treat".

They had a marvellous evening watching the Irish jigs. The partakers ages ranged from as young as five up to about eighty. The little children looked splendid in their green costumes.

After the dancing was over they had a number of folk singers appearing. The Irish really knew how to enjoy themselves. One would have thought that Shaun was a local as he was so well known. One man who was present on the previous night that she and Shaun were together, said to Shaun, "Ah, you have brought your lovely girl friend with you again that sung 'At Home in Donegal' like an angel".

The house was quiet when they got back, except for the dog wanting a fuss made of him.

Shaun assisted Mary in taking off her jacket and turned her round to face him. He said softly, "Mary, you don't know how much I have missed you".

"I've missed you too", she answered honestly as he drew her against him gently.

She needed Shaun badly and felt safe in his arms. He raised her face with his hand to receive his kiss and his lips held hers with a passionate significance.

Mary had found it difficult at first to cast Ron to the back of her mind. The many times that she had pined for him had caused her to make a conscious effort to supersede him with Shaun, dear Shaun, and she felt it was working. She eventually succeeded in not even dreaming of Ron any more, one needed hope to dream and there was no hope left. Yes, she convinced herself, she was gradually getting Ron out of her system and replacing him with Shaun.

In the morning after the exhibition there was a special delivery of the newspaper from the local newsagents. Everyone around there knew of Shaun's whereabouts, he was highly respected in the community and their hero.

Kevin read aloud the article on Shaun as the rest of them

all tucked into a hearty Irish breakfast.
The caption read:

'The Magical Master'
Shaun McGready, the successful lad from Newry, who spends a lot of his time painting around our lovely shores and hills of Donegal, staged yet another successful exhibition of his works in Dunfanaghy, attracted interest from discerning art lovers.

There were no duplicates among his work. Each is a limited edition, an original work of art in colour, produced personally by the artist and signed.

Buyers were offered a comprehensive collection, a subtle evocation of lazy summer days and some of the most popular images made an exorbitant sum of money. He is at his most inventive conjuring up tones of colours undreamt of by the normal run of the mill artist.

When interviewed yesterday at the exhibition, Mr McGready said, "I have always loved painting and never fail to have a marvellous feeling of gratification at seeing my work exhibited".

He was accompanied by an up and coming young artist, Mary Lavery, who displayed a definite flair. One of her paintings was of our very own Manor here in Falcarragh, which sold within minutes of the Gallery opening.

Mary waved Kevin and Katie off on their break to Dublin, they were like two children. She had never known that Katie had such a sparkling personality, she was a different person since she and Kevin had got together.

As they approached the reservation desk in the Dublin hotel, Kevin looked at Katie and asked, "Do you know Katie you have taken me back into your life, even accepted my proposal of marriage. The question I am going to ask you now is, are you going to go to your marriage bed morally chaste?".

Katie looked young and very eager, blushing like a teenager she answered, "Not if I can help it".

Kevin threw his head back and laughed saying humorously, "Damn it, I can't give our names as Mr Casey and Miss McGrath at our ages, I'll have to say Mr and Mrs Smith".

Her eyes shone as he turned round and winked slyly at her and she overheard him register them in the name of Mr and Mrs Kevin Casey.

Kevin and Katie were allocated a bedroom on the third floor. As they entered Katie eyed the massive big double bed straight away. The cover and frilled pillowcases were of an eye-catching spring bouquet design. It was set off with a matching master canopy attached to the wall, creating a four poster effect. All those years of fantasising not to mention the months of craving for him so close by in the study downstairs was now a reality; not only did she feel nervous, she was scared stiff and defenceless.

Kevin lightheartedly threw himself on the bed. "This is luxury, Katie, we'll get the best night's sleep we've ever had".

I certainly hope not, thought Katie, as she immediately started to unpack and hang up her dresses. She wanted him badly but was, on top of all the other feelings, very, very shy.

Kevin got off the bed, kicked off his shoes, flung his jacket and tie haphazardly over a chair then turned on the television. An old repeat of Deputy Dog was on; he threw himself back on the bed again and settled down to watch it.

He fell about laughing at the comical antics on the screen. Suddenly Katie was fuming; the last thing she wanted to see after twenty four years of sexual abstinence was Deputy Dog. She watched him intently for a while; her shyness suddenly allayed as at last it hit her - why, he was more nervous than she was; after all these years of being the stumbling block, she was going to have to do the seducing and her credentials were clearly lacking in that area.

With a prolonged action, she plugged in the kettle and arranged the cups and saucers methodically on the tray. She then hung her cardigan neatly on a hanger and slipped out of her shoes and tights before turning off the television. "Shall we have coffee before or after?". It was the best she could do.

He looked at her, she was beautiful, enticing and sexy - he rose to the bait; holding out his eager arms to her he replied in a husky voice, "After".

Clothes come off very fast after twenty four years of yearning. Caressing expert fingers and lips set their bodies aflame. With a deep and long overdue desire they communicated their need of each other and made love as if they were the most experienced lovers in the world.

The exquisite tremors were no sooner quelled when Kevin yelled breathlessly, "Katie, what did you turn the tele' off for? I'll miss the end of Deputy Dog".

Katie, drained of energy, manoeuvred herself in the direction of the television; twenty four years ago they might just have started all over again; but alas, time had taken its toll; they could very well have the best night's sleep they ever had.

Mary left the paper aside after scanning it and only by chance the name R A Casey caught her eye. She picked it up again and read the heading *'Residential Elderly Person's Home saved by Property Developer'*. She read on:

Mr R A Casey, of Casey Property Trust, saved Ardaragh House from closure. The 32 residents and 21 staff learned of the donation of £60,000 needed to save the home last night and celebrated by drinking a toast to their saviour. Mr Raymond Kelsop, the Chairman of the home said the decision to donate the money to the home was taken by Mr Casey after he had read of their plight in the local paper.

'The article had warned that short of a miracle the home was due for closure within a month'.

Many residents were in tears after the decision and worried about their immediate future. We tried to reassure them that we would find the best possible place for them but they were inconsolable. The home had lost £8,000 a year since 1987 and £60,000 was needed urgently for maintenance and to keep the home open. If it hadn't been for Mr Casey's kind donation the home would definitely have closed. Mr Casey has accepted an offer to visit the home on Tuesday morning in order to be thanked personally by the residents.

She put the paper down and wondered about his financial state, it was only a short time ago she read that his company was not doing as well as it could have done. She fished the cutting out of her handbag and read it again. It read; *Casey Property Trust, one of the biggest property companies in the South East, yesterday added their voice to the chants of woe facing many property developing companies.*

Announcing interim pre tax profits down 12% to £25.4m, Casey said it would be difficult to repeat the last full year's result of £75m. Mr Casey said there were very few opportunities to make profits from selling buildings. He added, the company, though obviously buffeted, is in a solid position with rentals continuing to produce good cash flow.

She threw the cutting in the fire and thought to herself, I'm not a damn bit interested in the man or his charity giving and company figures. She promptly set about preparing herself to look forward to Shaun's visit.

Ron's mother rang him to his office in London and told him that Jack, his step father was ill. The last few times Ron had visited, Jack had been feeling under the weather and the slightest thing tired him out. Ron advised him to have a checkup but Jack insisted he was alright and in need of nothing more than a tonic.

Belinda got worried and insisted he go along to the doctor even if it was only to get that tonic that he thought he needed. The result of the blood tests came through and proved that he had an incurable form of leukaemia. She didn't want to alarm Ron at the time, but he was now bed bound and failing fast. Ron, who had usually a tough disposition broke down on the phone and cried, "I will come as soon as I can, I will get the next flight".

Belinda was waiting for him and he immediately held out his arms to her and they comforted each other. "The doctor has been in and out today giving him pain killing injections. Brace yourself, he is not the man you knew", she warned him before going into the bedroom. Ron went into the room where Jack was propped up in bed. He took a look at the pathetic man in the bed and his heart broke. Jack had been a big healthy man with the strength of an ox and now he was reduced to a shadow.

"I am so glad you could come, I know you are a busy man", he said, chivalrous even now. Ron took his hand, there was no strength in his grasp.

"Your mother wants to tell you something, Ron, that should have been disclosed to you years ago", he said weakly.

"There is plenty of time for telling Ron, you get some sleep now Jack", said Belinda.

"I'd rather you would tell him now, as I never know whether I'll wake up again out of one of these drugged sleeps".

Belinda touched his forehead with her hand, checking his temperature and admired this courageous man she had devoted her life to.

She started to speak and came straight to the point, "Jack is your father, Ron. I became pregnant and Kevin married me thinking the child was his. You see Jack was two years younger than me, only a schoolboy. Kevin was always after me and although I liked him a lot, my love was for Jack. When I realised I was pregnant by Jack, I enticed Kevin into making love to me, which wasn't that difficult as he was besotted with me at the time. Then I told him about a month later I was pregnant, and he, honourably, to the delight of my parents, married me.

"I never stopped loving Jack and because of that my marriage to Kevin was a complete failure".

Ron was shocked by this news and fell down on his knees beside Jack and said slowly, "I forgive you but it was wrong of you both to keep that from me, I should have been told. I love you, Jack, and nothing could ever have changed that, I knew no other father".

The man who's name he had inherited wasn't his father after all. How on earth could he tell Kevin, after all these years? He simply couldn't.

Jack died peacefully in Belinda's arms the following day.

Chapter Nine

"Would I be rushing you in asking you to be my wife?".

The question was no surprise to Mary as she looked straight into Shaun's eyes. They were kind eyes and although it wasn't the most romantic of proposals, she knew he loved her and was certain she could learn to love this man in return. They had so much in common, they were good for each other, laughed together, they worked well together and they would be a great team together.

She answered slowly but surely with conviction, "I will be honoured to marry you, Shaun".

Shaun swept her into his arms and said excitedly, "You have made me the happiest man alive, I love you so much; let's make it soon".

His happy mood was infectious, she laughed and cried as she held him to her. If it is the last thing I do, I am going to see that Shaun remains happy for the rest of his life, she vowed.

Shaun's voice broke into her thoughts, "By the way, Mary, I'm exhibiting some work in Paris shortly, I'm not certain yet of the exact timing?".

"Oh, I've wanted you to come to Paris for so long, I'm delighted, I can't wait". she said with real enthusiasm, as she gave him an extra special hug.

On their return Katie and Kevin were delighted to hear of Shaun and Mary's decision to get married.

"We are so happy for you!", Katie said hugging them both in turn, "Which of us are going to get married first?"

Mary, quick to notice their radiant new found closeness associated with lovers said, "You are of course, you've waited long enough".

Kevin popped the champagne bottle and they all cheered. Although he was happy for Mary, he couldn't help feeling sad for Ron. If ever a man loved a woman, Ron loved Mary. He could have sworn that Mary loved him too but woman were unforgiving creatures, Katie had scorned him for years for one little misdemeanour.

The phone rang and as Mary was nearest she answered it, "I'm sorry, I can't hear you", and she turned around and said, without covering the phone, "Cut out the excitement you lot, I can't hear a thing". She spoke into the phone saying, "I'm sorry about the racket, who is speaking please?".

"It's Ron, I don't know what you are all celebrating there, but I'm certainly not celebrating", then added, unable to disguise the heartbroken tone in his voice, "My stepfather died today".

"I will put you straight on to your father", said Mary unable to convey the sympathy she felt for him.

Kevin spoke to Ron, "My God! Jack Murrey! Please

accept my deepest sympathy and convey it also to Belinda. He was a grand fellow! Yes, a grand fellow. He'll be sadly...". His voice faded away as they slipped out and Mary shut the door of the living room and left him to talk to Ron.

She felt badly shaken after hearing Ron's voice, especially as it reflected the same broken tone as on the occasion he left her that last day. Shaun put his arm around her for comfort and said, "Death is a sad occasion, don't I know it!".

Mary thought of his dead wife and held him close with heart-warming tenderness and hoped he would never be put through any further grief.

Katie and Kevin were married quietly and although Katie would have liked Mary and Shaun to be present at their wedding she accepted Mary's request to have Ron and Corrina as guests instead.

It was a very small affair with roughly fifty guests. Ron made a witty speech referring to the slow pace of the Irish: *'After negotiations extending over a period of twenty four years, a definite and satisfactory settlement has at last been reached. Going by the look on Katie's face, in a hot bed of fire tonight, she will prove to Kevin the error of his twenty four years of bachelor ways'*.

He toasted their happiness and read the telegrams then sat down.

Corrina piped up, "Ron, you have missed one".

He slowly got to his feet, steadied his voice and read. '*To Kevin and Katie the finest couple in the world. Have a wonderful life together. We are both looking forward to seeing you at our wedding whenever we have time for it. Everyone present raise your glasses and toast Kevin and Katie. Love and kisses, Mary and Shaun*'.

There was a unanimous toast to Kevin and Katie. Then Kevin stood up with a raised glass and said, "To Mary and Shaun". Everyone but Kevin and Katie were oblivious to the fact that Ron didn't raise his glass.

A week later while Mary was on her lunch break reading an English newspaper her eyes fell on an item in the announcements column.

Casey - Bonnington. Congratulations to Ronald and Corrina on your engagement. With love from Mum, Dad and Karen.

She tore the bit of paper off and crunched it in her hand, until her nails drew blood in her palm.

Ron and Corrina took a stroll through the park, then sat side by side on a bench making the most of their infrequent meetings in London together. Unobserved, Corrina studied Ron's face, he was a million miles away. Was this the face of a man newly engaged and from all accounts wanting to be married very soon? Early in their relationship he laughed a lot and used to tease her about how she could warm the cockles of his heart. Once he pulled her into his arms saying, "If I hadn't met you when I did, I was in great danger of becoming a boring old workaholic like my father". He had told her, on a previous occasion, that his father had been badly treated by some woman in the past and had little or nothing to do with women again. The woman turned out to be Katie, but she still didn't know what the break-up was about, nor did Ron. He had changed lately; he had something on his mind, but didn't feel it was worthy of a discussion. She thought his business was in a reasonable state but could be mistaken as he kept ploughing money into one venture after another and never mentioned the returns. At this precise time he was in the process of building luxury homes in Florida. She had gone along to one of the promotional evenings, to help with the presentation, but they didn't secure one sale. That evening he gesticulated by pursing his lips and saying, "That's the way it is, sometimes you win, sometimes you lose, today the famine, tomorrow the feast".

She would marry him because she loved him but she wished he would show more enthusiasm. In her heart she intuitively knew that he was a man of great passion and she longed for the time when she could awaken that fervent desire in him.

In turn, Ron's thoughts were never far from Mary. He constantly racked his brains as to why she had a total, full-scale change of heart. He just couldn't fathom her actions. He hadn't the slightest idea to what he could apportion the blame. She said it wasn't Corrina and he had been inclined to believe her. Unless it was of course that she felt sorry for McGready because of his unfortunate past, she couldn't possible love that unsightly, aggressive Irishman who held up his fists at the slightest provocation. To contemplate marrying a man one didn't love was akin to killing him with a knife instead of a gun. She had said it was her word against his, her word being that she didn't love him, and his, that she did. When was this woman going to stop making him boggle his mind with tortured logic. He couldn't admit to himself that there was no logic in continuing to work an argument to death.

He looked at Corrina; her large eyes, veiled with thick black eyelashes, were semi-transparent. The beauty of the woman never failing to amaze him. Today she looked delightful dressed in a beige jacquard cotton pullover which showed off the fullness of her round breasts, with a multi coloured necklace falling gently over them. Her belted beige trousers with a soft sheen hugged her slim figure to perfection. If ever a woman deserved better, it was she. It never entered his head that the logic he had applied to Mary marrying Shaun out of pity could indeed be applied to himself marrying Corrina on the rebound.

"When are you and I going to agree a wedding date, my diary is reasonably clear at the middle of next month".

"I'm booked up with the Paris Convention then, the first week in the following month would suit me better", Corrina replied.

"Very well, I'll cancel my bookings for that week and see

if we can get it arranged for then".

Mary enjoyed her work in central Paris and very often had a lunchtime meeting with her Director. She didn't have to use her French on these occasions as he spoke perfect English. Michel was pointing out a few items on a sheet of paper for Mary to deal with that afternoon when suddenly a voice rang out. "Mary! Why, Mary Lavery! How lovely to see you". She looked up to see Corrina Bonnington as she stopped short in her tracks. She looked sensational in a stylish, sand coloured suit. "Corrina, how lovely to see you, what are you doing here?".

"I'm trying to sell some damn computers to some damn Frenchmen, and they are as tight fisted as hell, don't want to part with a franc".

Michel stood up smiling as Mary introduced them. Then he said, "I will give you thirty minutes of my time. 3 O'clock sharp - if you can convince me, that I need your type of computer, in that time, I will convince you that all Frenchmen are not tight fisted".

As he walked off Corrina said, "Whoopee! I just might do it, and, what a dishy man".

Mary laughed, then said, "What have you on for tonight Corrina? I am happy to see you later if you wish".

"That will be marvellous, at the moment I have only the four walls in my hotel room on the agenda".

Mary had to rush but left her card stating the office address and told her to be on the dot for her appointment as Michel was a stickler for punctuality and they would arrange where to meet up after her meeting.

Corrina arrived at the office at 3.10pm, puffing and panting and ranting on about some last minute hitch. Mary showed her into Michel's office.

Michel gave her exactly twenty minutes. She stepped out of his office in a radiant mood, giving Mary the thumbs up before he emerged.

"Mary, I can't make up my mind which of the two I rate your friend best at, an accomplished sales woman or a computer expert", said Michel smiling.

"Well I hope I'm a bit of both, you see I just hate to see people use an out-dated computer that is as quaint as a hand-cranked wall telephone, in the assumption of prudence, while in fact the up to date technology could make them a considerable fortune".

Michel threw back his head and laughed, then composing himself, he took her hand in a firm handshake saying, "I am looking forward to meeting you this evening. As we arranged, I will pick you up at 7.30".

Mary accompanied Corrina to the revolving doors at the front of the building. She congratulated her on her engagement and in turn Corrina showed Mary her diamond cluster ring. "It's beautiful", she said, her smile hopefully covering her dismal feelings. She was not envious of the priceless ring as she sported a unique specimen of antiquity on her own finger which Shaun insisted on buying her as he knew she loved it the minute she saw it. Corrina congratulated Mary warmly in return as she admired the ring. "I hear Shaun is a great fellow, the four of us should try to get together some time".

Mary didn't know who informed Corrina that Shaun was a great fellow, one person she knew for certain it wasn't, was Ron. The thought of Ron and Shaun getting together was ludicrous as she knew it would test their endurance to the limit to even pass each other in the street.

Corrina mentioned that Ron would be in Leeds for a few days the following week, assisting Kevin and Katie in the completion of selling Kevin's home as they had decided to settle in Donegal.

Before they parted Corrina hugged Mary and said, "I'm sure you are pleased, that as things have turned out, you no longer have to devote your evening to me". She went on to add, "What a bit of luck running into you today, Mary! The reason I am meeting up with Monsieur Guerrin this evening is to demonstrate a compact computer to his son also to discuss in more detail the business computer he is interested in".

Mary had hoped to go to Donegal the following week but since she heard that Katie and Kevin would be away and she knew that Lucy would be there taking over, she instead rang Mrs Thompson and asked her if she knew the whereabouts of Sally. Mrs Thompson said, "My, what a coincidence, Sally called to see me last week and told me that as soon as she was settled she was going to get in touch with you. She started a new job in London this week. Hold on Mary and I'll get you her office phone number, unfortunately I haven't got her London address yet".

After a pleasurable chat with Mrs Thompson, Mary rang the number she had been given.

Sally was overjoyed to hear Mary's voice on the end of the line and although she would be working she thought it was a marvellous idea for Mary to visit her.

When Mary arrived the following week they had a terrific time exchanging their individual news bulletins of the past months. Mary and Sally had been best friends from tots. Sally was like a makeshift sister to Mary.

"He sounds marvellous this man you are engaged to", said Sally, then, true to her old form asked, "He hasn't got a brother by any chance?".

"He is marvellous", smiled Mary, "No, to the latter, but he may have a cousin".

"The probability of me finding an unattached attractive male is as likely as spotting a terrific bargain on the last day of Harrods sale", said Sally in a lighthearted fashion.

Mary had two days to push in before Sally would be off work for the weekend. She decided to do a few places of interest, and she had never been to Madam Tussauds.

On Wednesday she walked down Kensington High Street, satisfied that Ron was miles away when her heart missed a beat as she spied him walking towards his flat oblivious to everything but his newspaper. He steered himself in the right direction while he read something of interest, stopped, read for a few seconds, then just as suddenly folded the newspaper, lifting his head and looked her straight in the eyes. She was caught in the most uncompromising fashion, with her back against the lamppost holding in her breath as if it might be heard if she expelled it.

He was first to break the silence, "Do you want me for anything?".

"No".

"Then what are you doing outside my door?" he asked mercilessly.

"I am not outside your door, I am walking down the street minding my own business, anyway, I thought you were in Leeds".

Ron threw the girl one last look of condemnation, then without another word he turning his back on her, opened the door and closed it behind him.

He had the whip hand and God how it hurt. Her eyes blinded with tears she stumbled unto the road to the screeching of brakes.

A crowd gathered round her, as she lay on the road. She

couldn't breathe. Then she felt herself being helped to her feet and a familiar voice saying, "Give her space!". She had been buffeted and was winded but otherwise alright. The voice continued, "It's alright. I know her, I'll look after her".

"Are you alright my dear? Do you know him?", a kindly woman asked as she handed Mary her handbag.

"Yes, thank you", Mary replied as Ron ushered her into his flat.

"Holy Christ! Did you have to throw yourself under a bus?", he said as he settled her into a seat. Then he spoke with more concern, "Are you sure you are alright?".

"Yes, I'm fine, just unnerved".

He left her and came back with a strong brandy and held it to her lips. She sipped it obediently.

She removed the glass from her lips and blurted out, "Just because I can't love you, it shouldn't necessarily follow that you have to hate me".

He lowered himself into the seat opposite her and said in disbelief, "I don't hate you! But what is the implication of that? You want me to be your friend, do you? Which in fact means you want me also to shake McGready by the hand and congratulate him on winning the woman I love. If that is what you are asking of me, a mere mortal, then I am sorry I can not deliver".

"I don't think we could ever be friends either... I just never want to see that look of loathing in your eyes, I haven't done anything to warrant it", she answered in a low inarticulate voice.

She forced herself to look him straight in the eyes, wondering if she dare tell him the truth; he would probably take it badly but which was the worst of two evils; the fact that she didn't love him or that she couldn't ever love him. The perpetuity of it was similar.

He became fascinated with the unusual colour of her eyes, they had intrigued him before on occasions, and for the life of him he couldn't think where he had seen them before. They were dark brown with a blue hue but this wasn't the time or place to fathom it out, it would come to him some day.

He held out his hand to her, he didn't compel her to reciprocate, the onus was on her. She lifted up her left hand and put it into his right extended hand and they held unto each other for dear life almost as if they were giving each other the power of endurance. He couldn't know what was going through her mind, nor she his, but they were both wary of being the one to break the inspiring spell.

He inadvertently broke the enchantment with words that brought her back to the harsh reality of it all by saying, "It's not too late for us, Mary!".

She withdrew her hand and said, "It is too late, it is and always will be, inconceivable".

"Can you, in all honesty, assure me that is your final word ?".

"Absolutely and completely", she answered steadily, feeling she had stripped the last crumb of dignity from him, but had no other choice.

The transformation in Ron was instantaneous, it was as if all those months had been wiped out, from the moment he had touched her in the garden up until a few minutes ago when he had infused life into her.

He held his head high and said, "Very well, you need never have any further worries of me hassling you. For the sake of my father and Katie, if not for ourselves, I suggest we discontinue playing cat and mouse. Although I wholeheartedly agree with you we can never be friends, there is no reason for us to be enemies".

"Thank you", she said humbly.

He walked to the phone, dialled a number and said, "Karen, when have I a free moment tomorrow?". After a pause he said, "Pencil in Miss Lavery".

Mary was dismissed, he held the door open for her, saying, "Be at my office at 11.30 in the morning, I have a proposition to make to you".

"But what ... ?".

He stifled her question curtly saying that he would explain then and she had already kept him late for an appointment this afternoon.

The following evening when Sally came in from work, Mary told her she had an offer of a job, she couldn't refuse and went on to tell her all about it.

"That is absolutely wonderful, Mary, it certainly is a celebrating matter. Let's go somewhere special tonight and the champagne is on me".

Mary still couldn't quite take it in. Ron had offered her twice the salary she was on now and the best part of it was, it was a challenging job that she would love doing.

She had no idea what Ron wanted to see her about, just a hint of a suspicion. She felt good about her appearance as she was shown into his large bright office, overlooking Marble Arch. Her eyes immediately ascended to the painting on the wall. Her painting of the Manor: It looked magnificent now that it was segregated from Shaun's masterpieces. She looked at the pencilled signature with pride.

"Sit down, Mary", Ron said, omitting a greeting.

He got straight to the point, "Mary, as you know, the Château De Montville is undergoing vast changes and we are aiming to get it ready for new tenants by Christmas. Taking all the costs into consideration, it is vital that we get some prompt returns. I am offering you the job, right from the start, in unearthing the type of people out there requiring what we have to offer."

Mary gaped at him, not as yet been given the chance to open her mouth.

He went on, "When I came back from France, I decided I wanted a bright, young, energetic, self-starter with a professional approach, must be a confident communicator, able to make winning presentations and foster excellent business relationships with the customers. Well, I believe you have the qualities I am looking for and will be able to meet the challenges".

It all went over the top of her head, in one ear and out the other. That was the effect this man had on her. Although she hadn't taken in the elaborate essentials required for the position, she knew she was offered the job of getting the tenants for the Château De Montville, and she wanted it.

"Ron, I am indeed honoured that you have offered me the job but it would be wrong of me to accept before I talk to Shaun,as we haven't discussed the prospect of me holding down a career".

"Corrina is a career woman, I wouldn't expect her to end that just because she was getting married. In your case it wouldn't be a long term job, it would be more in the line of an assignment, even McGready wouldn't expect you to pass over such an opportunity".

Mary mused aloud, "I will have to give at least two weeks notice and getting married will take a few weeks, I can't see me being in a position to take it up for about six weeks".

"This is no time for frivolity, it is serious business, if you can't start in two weeks time, I will have to get someone else, it is vital we get the show on the road".

"Very well, I will start in two weeks", she said, "I will work two weeks notice and will sort out the other frivolous matter somehow".

He held out his hand to her and they shook hands in a business like fashion, "Obviously you will report directly to me. There will be occasions that you need company support on business trips and guidance, my deputy, Keith Lawson, will fill that role. You need never have any worries about you and I being thrown together for days".

Mary lay looking at the ornate ceiling in Sally's flat, feeling a bit on the tipsy side after being out on the town celebrating. Her mind was in a jumble, she never did hear why Ron was in London when he should have been with Kevin and Katie in Leeds. Also she still hadn't a clue how to tell Shaun, but she closed her eyes and mumbled, "I'll think of that tomorrow".

Chapter Ten

Shaun arrived in Paris at 10.30 on Friday morning. He decided not to ring Mary at her office and would surprise her when she got home from work. He let himself into the flat with the spare key she had sent him and went straight through to the kitchen. The first thing that caught his eye was an envelope against the coffee percolator. It had Sally written across the front. She was obviously expecting Sally to come in before her and he wondered if she was working late. He decided to ring her office, simply to check her whereabouts and he could easily ask whoever he spoke to not to mention he rang.

The receptionist answered with the company name, "Michel Guerrin, Bonjour".

Shaun said, "Bonjour, Mademoiselle", then in English, prompting her to reply in English, he asked if Miss Lavery was in the office, to which she replied, "I'm sorry, Miss Lavery left our employment last week".

Shaun was surprised but asked calmly, "Could you tell me where I can contact her please?".

"I'm sorry, I am unable to help you".

Shaun went through to the lounge to gather his thoughts together when he heard a key in the lock. A young blond girl walked in and stopped dead as she saw him.

"Who are you, how did you get in?", she asked in alarm.

"I am Shaun, you must be Sally, there is a note in the kitchen for you".

Sally's face lit up and came forward with her hand outstretched, "Oh, I am pleased to make your acquaintance, I have heard so much about you".

Shaun shook her hand vigorously and said, "Same goes for me. Obviously Mary is expecting you but I was going to surprise her".

Sally rushed through to the kitchen to get the note and came out again and gave the written page to Shaun. He read -

Sally, I am really sorry I had to go off on business at short notice. I missed you at the office, you had already left when I rang. I hope you can occupy yourself for the weekend. I will make it up to you somehow. Please forgive. Mary.

Sally said, "Mary came to stay with me three weeks ago and we arranged for me to visit this weekend".

Shaun spoke perplexedly, "The tables have turned on me, she is the one to surprise me especially as I didn't even know that she had changed her job".

"I'm sorry, Shaun, I know she didn't want to worry you about the fact that she was going to have to postpone the wedding for a while. Don't worry about anything until you talk to her".

They both wondered what they should do in the circumstances. Shaun said, "I have an exhibition to attend tomorrow morning, I will book into a hotel".

"No, of course you will not, I will take myself back to London, I have an open return flight ticket", Sally insisted.

"Do you really want to go back though? I am quite happy to have you accompany me in the morning to the exhibition gallery, that is, if you are interested of course".

Sally's eyes lit up, "I can't believe it, I am being invited by the renowned Shaun McGready to accompany him to one of his exhibitions!", she exclaimed with rapturous admiration.

Shaun laughed heartily, "Well, believe it, I'm happy to have you".

They decided neither of them would move out. Shaun took the guest room and Sally, Mary's room.

Ron had asked Mary to hold onto her flat in Paris until an office and suite could be set up for her in the Château De Montville. She had a meeting with him and Keith Lawson on her first day at work, but since that day she hadn't any more dealings with him. For the first three days she worked closely with Keith, a fifty year old, who was on his second career after taking an early retirement package from a large company in Cheshire. Mary and he felt they would make a good team on the occasions when they had to work together. She had been prepared to spend her first week in London but had hoped to be in Paris at the weekend for Sally's arrival. As it happened she had to fly back to Paris then return to London for a five day training course that Keith arranged for her at short notice. It was customary for raw recruits to attend this course.

She had spoken to Shaun on the phone every third night for the last three weeks and for the life of her couldn't bring herself to tell him of her new job, also because she was going to have to delay the wedding for a while and partly because of he and Ron's mutual dislike of each other. It was only a week ago that Shaun had said, "Don't you think it's getting near time we started making wedding arrangements? I can't stand to be apart from you my sweetheart". She told him she was in agreement with him and they would talk about it when next they met.

They were a friendly lot of training consultants and everyone on the course thoroughly enjoyed it and agreed it had been remarkably instructional. They covered an enormous amount and were laden down with notes and books at the end of it. She had an advantage over some of the others in the fact that she was able to take notes in shorthand. She flicked through a few pages on the plane on the way back to Paris then started to read some of the notes:

- We have to provide greater customer satisfaction if we are to get ahead. Customers have become more demanding and of course competition is increasing.

- We expect you not to raise expectations by saying you

will sort out their problems before checking that it can be fixed and never make a promise unless you can fulfill it.

- Set yourself a specific goal, enter into competition with yourself. Do not work harder, work more intelligently and better.

- Eye contact is vital, there is no point in smiling at your foot, your foot isn't your client. Enjoy your customers, they pay your wages.

She closed her eyes; she was dead tired but knew that when she got home she wouldn't be able to let the stuff lie, being so keen.

Ron had done her a twofold good turn, she hadn't time to dwell on her personal tragedy. They had both agreed they could never be friends, but perhaps as colleagues, they would get on reasonably well.

When she arrived at the flat she was confronted with two envelopes resting against the coffee percolator.

"Oh my God! My God!", she said as she read them consecutively.

My Darling Mary
I decided to spring a surprise on you, but it back-fired. It was the weekend of my Paris exhibition and it went very well, all sold out, a few more coppers towards our new home.

Congratulations on your new job, your friend Sally didn't

tell me the name of the company but she said it was a good job and you were very excited about it. Of course, my darling, I want to marry you soon, but only when the timing is right for you.

By the way you have a good friend in Sally and from the word go we hit it off.

Please don't make it too long till we meet again. I look forward to hearing your sweet voice on the phone. Love Shaun.

Dear Mary
I accept your apology but obviously I was sorry you were not here at the weekend. That new job of yours looks like it is going to be demanding.

I hope you don't mind that I spent the weekend with Shaun. He is everything you said and more. You know how mad I am on history, well he is going to send me some literature on the history of Ulster. He told me a little, he has a great flair for words, I could listen to him all day and never get bored. If he was mine, I'd be as jealous as hell if he spent a day with another woman but you don't need to worry as he is besotted with you, worst luck. No, he hasn't got an eligible cousin! - ha!

Hope we meet soon, in the meantime I will ring you. Love Sally.

Mary rang Shaun straight away, it was late but she couldn't put it off until tomorrow. He answered in a non too pleased hoarse voice, he had been fast asleep. When he heard Mary's voice, he became more alert, "Darling, how are you, have you just arrived back?".

They didn't speak long until the crucial question came. She took a deep breath then answered steadily, "Casey Property Trust".

There was a long silence then he spoke gruffly, "You are not expecting me to be overjoyed about this, are you?".

"No darling, I don't expect that, but I want you to please understand that this is a challenging job for me, the man is secondary. I didn't particularly want to be a secretary, well not for long anyway, I wanted to eventually use the business part of my degree and I feel I am now on sure ground".

Shaun's words came down the line, "I don't know whether you know it or not but I am a rich man and you need never work".

"Shaun, why don't you try to understand, I'm not money orientated, I need a sense of achievement". She then went on to repeat what Ron had said to her about it only being an assignment.

His voice came back with a worried tone, "I'm not sure that I can put up with this insular arrangement much longer, are you sure there won't be another assignment after this, and then another?".

"No, darling, I want children and being an only child

myself, I mean children, plural".

Shaun lay back on his pillow, his voice softened considerably, "Alright, my darling, you have my support in this. I love you very much, I wish you were here now, tucked in beside me".

"I love you too", said Mary. She left down the phone convincing herself that everything would be alright.

Mary settled into her office in the ground floor of the Château De Montville. She was pleasantly surprised at how well the flats had turned out, the windows had all been double glazed and fitted carpets throughout. The interior designers had done a great job and she was impressed at the good quality of the workmanship.

She was conscientious at work and tenants were secured for two of the self contained luxury flats. She had talked through with Keith on the phone, the idea of one month's free rental on long term rentals of a year or over. He told her he thought it was a terrific idea and to go ahead and advertise the offer. The type of people that took on these flats were in the well off bracket, but it is surprising what a free offer can do.

Keith was accompanying her next Wednesday at meetings she had set up with a few large companies, that were expanding into the area. She was hopeful of securing a few more rentals. Company directors, on high salaries were her main business contacts. They were usually recruited for, at most, two years in the hope of turning companies around and were more likely to rent than buy as they very often had a home elsewhere. She must get through to them that renting gives flexibility without long-term commitment.

She wouldn't see Ron until the monthly meeting which was held on the first Thursday of every month. At that meeting, all the consultants responsible for rentals, sales and purchasing of properties, would get together to discuss their performance.

When Wednesday arrived Mary couldn't believe it when Ron rushed into her office. The surprise and disappointment must have shown on her face as he said, "I'm really sorry, Mary, but Keith couldn't make it today, he was rushed to hospital with an attack of appendicitis".

"Oh, I am sorry, I do hope he is alright", she said as she gathered up her briefcase and told Ron that they had to leave straight away.

"What, no time for coffee?".

"I'm afraid not", she said as she ushered him out to his car.

They had three meetings, one success. Ron smiled down at Mary as they left, "Well, it looks like it is coming together nicely, congratulations Miss Lavery. Dare I ask when it will be Mrs McGready?".

"It will be Miss Lavery for a little while yet I'm afraid", she replied.

Ron looked at his watch and said, "I have three hours until I make my way back to the airport. I am starving, I will find myself a restaurant. I would like to go over a few things with you so I will expect you to join me".

"I know my place, you are my boss and if you want to discuss today's meetings, then I will indeed join you", she said.

Ron thought she looked stunning tonight as she sat opposite him in the restaurant. She was wearing a black wool shift dress and ivory and black silk grosgrain jacket, but then he knew she looked stunning in anything she wore or indeed nothing at all. Although he was careful not to show any outward signs of affection for the girl, she still drove him crazy with desire.

It was a delicious and elongated meal that the French invariably go in for, so there was plenty of time to discuss business between courses.

Ron decided that was enough shop for the evening and said to Mary, "Corrina and I went to Donegal last weekend, my father is looking twenty years younger, after all he has gone through too".

Mary's eyes-lit up at the mention of Kevin, "I know, isn't it marvellous how he and Katie got together".

"They are wanting to buy the Manor you know, he says he will leave it to me in his will". They both laughed.

Corrina had told Mary that she and Ron were getting

married very quietly in a week or so. Mary had trained herself to feel no envy. It was almost like as if she were under hypnosis, she could demagnetise herself from Ron. Even now as she sat opposite him she was in that state of resistance.

"Mary, I am going to tell you something, it must be strictly off the record".

She hoped he wasn't going to tell her that his business was going under as that would have a harmful effect on her now.

"Kevin isn't my father, but I can't ever tell him".

He went on to tell of Jack's revelation before he died. Taking no notice of Mary's reaction and drinking the wine unwittingly right down to the dregs. He had wanted to divulge the information to someone but hadn't thought Corrina was the one and certainly not Katie.

"I do hope Jack knew I held him in the highest esteem. I don't think I could have shown him any more love even if I had known. It must have hurt him that I always called Kevin father and he, Jack, but it was what I had been brought up to believe".

Ron raised his head and looked at her, she was ashen faced as she slipped awkwardly to the floor in a heap.

She came round to the sounds of "Appelez une ambulance immédiatement!", and "comment ca va?".

"Pas d' ambulance s'il vous plâit", she managed to say to the waiter.

Ron steered her to the car, waving aside offers of help. "Are you alright?", he asked with concern.

"Yes thank you, the heat in places like that sometimes causes me to faint", she answered incoherently, she was still in a state of shock.

Ron wasn't exactly in the best state to drive, he must have taken more than his share of the wine, so he hailed a taxi back to the château. He had by now decided to get the early morning flight as the meal had gone on longer than he had anticipated.

The caretaker gave him a key of a room he could have for the night and he then escorted Mary to her suite to satisfy himself that she was alright. She stopped and faced him at the door saying, "I am absolutely fine there is no need for you to come in".

"I'll wait with you for ten minutes only, just to reassure myself".

When they were inside he asked her if she kept any brandy, to which she nodded to the cabinet.

He poured them both a small glass, saying, "This brandy business is getting to be a habit. Last time you threw yourself under a bus, tonight you drop at my feet like a rag doll. I seem to have a detrimental effect on you".

He saw her screw up her face at the strength of the brandy, and said, "Take a few sips it should get the colour back into your face and hopefully it will steady my nerves. I shouldn't have unloaded my problems on you especially as you weren't feeling well. I guess I was looking for a shoulder to cry on".

If Ron had been expecting a shoulder to cry on he had confided in the wrong person. She couldn't comfort him with words. God if he only knew, she needed comforting herself more than anything. The demagnetism that had protected her from him for so long had deserted her, she was in a worse position now with the disclosure of his parentage. Suddenly it all overwhelmed her and the tears came tumbling down her face, then with outstretched arms, she said, imploringly, "Oh Ron, please hold me!".

Ron looked at her but ignored her outstretched arms and backed off. The ambiguous warnings that he had been unaware of previously led him to believe he just couldn't cope with her in a demonstrative seductive mood, only to be cast aside in favour of McGready again. He was weak-kneed but resolute as he looked at her still ashen face and said, "I am not your plaything Mary when you feel like it, but I will lay my cards fair and square on the table. If you can say to me now in all honesty, that you don't love McGready, I will call off my wedding".

She looked at him with red rimmed eyes, disappointed that he had mistaken her need of comfort for being a deranged mistress, then unable to bear the interrogation of his eyes, as he waited for her to forsake Shaun, she turned her back on him.

She heard him gulp the last of the drink, put the glass on the table, then the click of the door as it closed behind him.

Are there any winners in this game, she thought. Is Shaun going to be a winner? My God, I hope so.

In the morning she splashed her eyes with cold water and lay back with cucumber on them; she had to face Ron looking as normal as possible. She might not have bothered, he was gone. He obviously preferred to hang round the airport for an hour rather than have a confrontation with her.

She hoped her job was safe, she loved it from the very first day. If there was a chance of encountering him every day of the week, then she would have had to look at it in a very different light, but as it was she felt she had no reason to leave and he should have no reason to get rid of her.

There were a few business points he had brought up last night, that needed further discussion, perhaps she should have checked with him today, but decided to use her own initiative.

She was wrong! He came on the phone later to discuss them, but she had already dealt with them. He said, "In this company, Mary, nothing must stand in the way of business. I must ask you to keep that policy in mind".

She apologised and he accepted her apology. When she put the phone down, she knew he was right. If she couldn't discuss business with him because of the way she felt about him, then there was no place for her here.

Corrina rang Mary the day before her wedding. She said, "I'm so sorry that you are unable to attend our wedding, Mary, Ron told me that you are tied into a very important meeting".

"Yes, but I do wish you all the happiness in the world", said Mary, composing her voice as best she could.

"I really would have liked you to have been there, but Kevin and Katie will be there of course".

Mary had actually bid her goodbye and good luck and had taken the phone away from her ear when she heard Corrina say urgently, "Oh Mary.. Hold on! Your old boss called into my office when in Chelmsford. I went out to lunch with him, he is delighted with the computers I sold him. He also asked after you, he said you were the best secretary he ever had. I think he is really nice, Mary, and I hope to keep in touch with him and his son".

Corrina replaced the phone and stretched out full length on the settee. She felt sick to the pit of her stomach, unable to get him out of her mind. If she didn't love Ron so much, she could go for that impressively flamboyant Frenchman in a big way. Yes, they had lunch together that day in Chelmsford, but what she didn't tell Mary was that she also had dinner with him in the evening.

It all started the night she went to his home in Paris.

After his son, Phillipe, with whom she had a lot of fun during the evening, had retired to bed, Michel embarked on a light-hearted flirtation. Visiting France in her line of business, she wasn't alarmed and was well used to dealing with enamoured Frenchmen. On that occasion she gave as good as she got, flirted back with an ease that astonished her.

He played fast that first evening and had the nerve to kiss her as he assisted her out of the car at the hotel, saying, "On peut se revoir?". When he asked if he could see her again, she knew he wasn't referring to business. She became slightly evasive and with much scepticism, at last responded that she hoped they would indeed meet again. After all she was depending on those sales.

He rang her at her Chelmsford home, she was flattered and eventually made an arrangement to meet up with him again when she was in Paris at the Computer Convention.

There was no doubt about it, she wouldn't be a woman if she hadn't been attracted to him. He had perfected the art of massaging one's ego.

"Does Casey love you as I love you?", he asked.

"Yes, in his way. He doesn't shout it from the roof tops, but that's the way English men are".

"He couldn't possibly love you as I love you. You completely fill my mind from the moment I wake up in the morning to my last thought at night. Then it all rotates again; I open my eyes and think of you".

His French accent may have attributed to her warm-hearted reaction. Yes, the guy certainly knew how to sweet-talk.

The day he came to Chelmsford specially to see her, though wholly irresponsible, she simply packed up work and spent the entire day with him.

In the evening they shared a romantic, candlelit dinner together at the hotel he was booked into. At the coffee stage he said to her, "Please come to my room! I promise you will come to no harm. I may kiss you to some romantic background music, but I swear that is all. I will neither expect nor demand anything more of you".

He had an unfair advantage over her, his smile was too damned alluring.

They skipped coffee in the restaurant and had it in his room.

True to his word, he inserted a compact disc, drew her into his arms to the faint strains of Mozart's 'concerto pour violon' and they spontaneously kissed.

As they kissed she felt his body move against her and was encircled, swallowed up and engulfed with passion. Then he set about breaking his promise. "Stay with me ma belle". he whispered tantalisingly in her ear.

Her mind became overloaded with unsolvable queries:

Could she love Ron and still want this man so

desperately? Was she abnormal in wanting him? Would it be all that wrong to have one night of love before committing herself to one man for the rest of her life? Men got off with this type of thing, why then shouldn't she? Damn it - Wasn't she a liberated woman? Why not?

Michel's breath had become sporadic and uneven as he waited for her reply. "My darling... ?" he prompted.

She released herself slightly from his strong grip and looked into his beseeching eyes.

"I'll stay with you, Michel, and do you know something? Even if you hadn't asked, I would have, because there is nothing at this moment in time I want more".

The memory of that night would stay with her forever. While they lay in each other's arms in a delicious feeling of contentment, he paid her one hell of a compliment. He had said, "Corrina, I don't want you to think that this is all I need of you. I love you more than I have ever loved anyone and your wedding day is going to be the worst day of my life". It had never been her intention for him to have become so emotionally committed to her and she cried in his arms as they made love: she didn't want to hurt him, but then she didn't want to hurt Ron either.

She rose from the settee with a sigh. Ah well, she was marrying another man tomorrow regardless of all that unbridled passion unleashed that night to a rush of sexual excitement. He had awakened a part of her that had been dormant for too long. God knows she had wanted him, still did, but these feelings would disappear tomorrow.

Ron would diminish and crush her longings for Michel Guerrin forever.

At the same moment in time Michel Guerrin sat at his desk awaiting his next client. He flicked through his notes with wandering attention. Another rich widow seeking the best investment and outlet for her deceased husband's hard earned cash.

His buzzer sounded. "Madame Crepeau to see you Michel", his not so new secretary announced.

"Annie, according to my notes I am expecting Madame Ernaux", said Michel tiresomely.

"You are correct. I am sorry. Shall I show her in?".
Why couldn't all secretaries be as efficient as Mary? Why did she have to leave him for that man? That man! Mon Dieu, that man!

Michel vacated his chair and met his client as she came through the door. "Bonjour, Madame Ernaux. Je vous en prie".

An hour later Michel made his way to a nearby cafe for a beer and a sandwich knowing every detail of her inheritance. He was already formulating ideas in his mind of how he would invest her five million francs to give her a tax efficient return. The trust and confidence that these rich widows placed in him at a first meeting never failed to amaze and exhilarate him. Today, however, it would take more than the prospect of a hefty commission to lift him out of the doldrums.

As he strummed his fingers on the table in agitation he wondered how she could love that man. He visualised her sitting across the table in the restaurant. Her beauty that night was indescribable: she was wearing a stunning stylish claret coloured suit with a black contrasting border. Her eyes shone with 'a-devil-may-care' look, and, dare he recall, a glimmer of love.

God knows he could get exotic woman by the score. Women were continually trying to bed him, but he had no more interest in them than that rich and beautiful widow he had just done business with. If he had time to bid these women time of day it was the height of it.

Corrina was head and shoulders above any woman he had ever met. I suppose he must have fallen for her on that first day when she called his prize computer as outdated as 'a cranked old wall telephone'.

His desire and obsession for her mounted when she spent two days in Paris at the Computer Convention. She spent time with him outside the Convention hours, but what she didn't know, was that he had wangled his way in to hear her address the delegates. God, what a woman!

What manner of man was Casey to keep his woman sex starved? She was like a young animal let loose on the opposite sex for the first time. After the preliminary exploration of each other's bodies, he entered her gently and with velvet smoothness, but she went wild. Later in the night she relaxed and became more calm and tender.

He grimaced agonisingly and dropped his head into his hands in despair as he visualised them together. It was unbearable to think of them. Would she cry in his arms with emotional gratification, not pity, as their bodies reached the frenzied limits of control?

He oppressively rose from the table, a bad taste in his mouth, the beer had become flat and bland in sympathy with his emotions.

Mary woke up on Ron's wedding day feeling jaded and the call from Corrina yesterday hadn't helped. She was devastated about the way things had turned out and the thought of Corrina, with all her beauty, standing together with Ron at the marriage ceremony, both smiling, almost drove her crazy. She knew she was torturing herself with these thoughts but couldn't stop.

She prepared herself for the day's meeting - the important meeting Ron had told Corrina she was tied into. It was no more vital than any other, every meeting was important as far as she was concerned.

As it happened she clinched her biggest deal yet, perhaps at the same moment in time as the wedding. She extended herself beyond her supposed capability and was thrilled beyond comparison as she felt the elation of achievement.

She had gained confidence and even had the strength of character to turn down the prospective tenants whom she knew were not suitable. She would do this if she could see that the customer was about to make a mistake out of ignorance and that what was on offer did not really suit their particular needs.

Mary got into Heathrow in good time and took a taxi to the office. She was first in the meeting room for the monthly convention and had no idea who would chair the meeting as Ron and Keith were both unavailable. She was going through her notes when Ron walked in and took her by surprise. In a state of disarray she half stood up, then sat down again awkwardly.

"Hello, Mary", he said, "You're early".

She didn't know whether to congratulate him or not, then decided against it and said, "Hello Ron, I came straight here as I had a few things to read up on".

They sat quietly both absorbed in their notes for a further ten minutes before the others arrived. Mary tried to remain unperplexed as they each in turn congratulated Ron and one of them slapped him on the back saying, "Well done, but how can you leave a delectable woman such as Corrina on your honeymoon?".

Ron made a non too genteel remark about how she exhausted him, he needed a break from it and they all laughed heartily.

"Right, enough is enough, we have a lady present". Only Mary detected the undertone in his voice as he said the word lady. A few of them apologised to her for the light-hearted banter. It was about as much as she could take but managed a half-hearted grin.

The meeting continued exuberantly throughout the day without a lunch-time break. They nibbled at the sandwiches the secretaries had brought in while still concentrating on the main issues.

Ron spoke to each of them in turn, giving them roughly ten minutes each. When he came to Mary he was brief and to the point, "Mary, you are doing a tremendous job for us, almost breaking our records in fact. Keep it up for a month then maybe you should have a change of scenery for a week or so. Keith will explain to you when he returns".

Mary was pleased that she was appreciated and was happy to await Keith's return to discover what her change of scenery was.

Chapter Eleven

Kevin wished Katie wouldn't worry so much about Mary. He tried to explain to her, without success, that she and Ron were sensible, intelligent adults and wouldn't have decided to work together unless they knew they could handle it. When they first met they discovered an instantaneous bond between them and mistook it for love, but in the light of day they have logically agreed they were mistaken and have settled for a companionable co-worker arrangement instead, which suits them both.

Katie listened to his logic over and over, she wished she could tell Kevin just how close that bond was, but knew that if ever he was to be told, it had to come from Mary herself.

The tears had streamed down Katie's face when the wedding between Ron and Corrina was taking place. She, and only she, knew that Ron loved Mary. He looked towards Katie just before he took the vows, it was a look of apology coupled with sorrow. That look made her feel so sorry for him that her tears come in abundance. Kevin had never known Katie to be so soft and handed her his handkerchief. "I can't help crying at weddings", she said.

Ron and Corrina looked the perfect couple. Corrina was exquisitely dressed in a crepe-de-chine suit in cream with a delicate floral design and a sweetheart neckline. She wore a single row of pearls on her neck and wrist. Her hat was a dream in silk cream and framed her black hair which fell around her face in curls in contrast to the straight style she normally wore.

Ron in turn looked handsome in a quality sand washed, single breasted suit, in a most unusual shade of wine. He wore a silk shirt in a muted floral shade.

The whole event had been stressful for Katie, if there had been any way she could have got out of it, she would have, but she felt she owed it to Kevin to attend. Belinda of course was present and it was the only time, over the course of the day, that Katie saw real love in Ron's eyes, when he had greeted his mother. In her observance she noticed him smile at Corrina quite a few times but it was a smile of the mouth that never quite reached his eyes.

Katie had convinced Kevin that he should retire now from the rat race and take it easy. He was still a relatively young man in his early fifties but he had worked harder than most men and he had made a lot of money. She was right, he could afford to take it easy. "If I retire will you promise to take up golf with me?", he said.

"Why not? I might even take up fishing", she answered with a laugh.

Katie and Kevin were very much in love; they were happier now than at any other time in their lives. If only Mary could find happiness, she thought, I would be the happiest person alive.

They were both looking forward to seeing Ron at the weekend, to discuss the prospect of them taking over the Manor and the probability of offering the cottage to

Alison and John with the option of the little business that went with it. Now that he was married to Corrina, he would never settle in Donegal, she had said she would never live out in the wilds. Ron had told them she was unable to accompany him this weekend due to a previous business arrangement.

Shaun was overjoyed to hear that Mary was coming at last to visit him in Newry. She had told him that she hoped he didn't mind but Sally would also spend one night with them.

He said, "Oh, I don't mind at all, she is a delightful girl and I know I shall enjoy giving her a history lesson, but I wouldn't like her to be here all of the time as I want you to myself very badly indeed".

"I need you so much too, my darling. I love my work but I can't go on sacrificing my private life in it's favour".

Sally had jumped at the invitation, "I am so looking forward to seeing you both again. I promise not to get in the way. You and Shaun will have a day together before I arrive and another when I leave".

When Mary rang to book her flight she was lucky, but surprised to hear that she had got the last seat on the plane and they were fully booked for the rest of the weekend.

She had a company car now and made her way to the airport in good time. It was an extremely hot day and was glad she had gone for the worthwhile extra of air conditioning which kept the car comfortable. She felt more alert in a cool environment and was also able to listen to tapes without the tiresome noise from open windows. She didn't mind solitary driving because it was an escape from the stresses of life. Her car was a decompression chamber, a place to meditate and she could indulge in replaying Don Williams over and over, which would drive other people mad if they were in her company.

Only a short distance down the motorway she ran into a severe hold up a few kilometres North East of the junction with the Peripherique towards Charles de Gaulle Airport. There was chaos in the whole region; she stood outside her car with many other protesting drivers; but there was nothing they could do. She couldn't even abandon her car and take a taxi as no traffic was getting through at all. The tears ran down her cheeks as she worried about what Shaun would think and she really wanted to see him badly to be reassured of his love.

It was midnight before she got back to the Château and dialled him. He told her he was devastated when she never got off the plane and spoke to others as they alighted and heard the disturbing news of the traffic chaos.

"Don't be upset my darling, there was nothing you could do about it. However, this episode tonight highlights the problem we have. I want to marry you soon so that we can be together all the time".

"Please don't let us go over that again, I want to marry

you but in a few months time. Surely we can both wait for a few months, you know it means so much to me".

"I suppose you are right, what are a few months, we will have the rest of our lives together", he said unconvincingly.

Then he remembered about Sally and said urgently, "What are we going to do about Sally? She is coming in first thing in the morning, do you think I should ring her at this late hour of the night ?"

"Oh Shaun, I am sorry, we can't ring her at 12.30, she will be fast asleep and knowing Sally, she will have all her clothes laid out ready for a quick getaway in the morning".

"Not to worry, I'll see she enjoys her weekend, but take note my darling, I am coming to France at the first possible opportunity I get".

Mary fell into bed that night exhausted and hoped Sally wouldn't be too disappointed.

Sally in turn was disappointed when she saw Shaun standing alone as she came through the customs and she knew he was putting on an act when he made light of it. "Ah well, you and I are going to enjoy ourselves regardless", he said.

"I'll drive you back to my house, then later I shall give you a grand tour of my lovely country".

Shaun lived in a sprawling modern ranch type bungalow, constructed in both mahogany and fine grained stone, up a tree lined lane, giving the impression of being an extremely peaceful haven. The interior was magnificent. Generously proportioned open airy rooms were thoughtfully furnished in contemporary style comfortable furniture. The modern kitchen and utility room was floored in Italian tiles.

"I am sure Mary loves this house", ventured Sally.

"This was to have been Mary's first visit here, she doesn't want to live in this part of Ireland, she would prefer to live in Donegal".

Sally wasn't at all sure if his words harboured a note of sadness.

"Today, I will take you to some of the areas round about, but tomorrow we will go further afield", said Shaun.

"I won't be here tomorrow, I am leaving early in the morning".

"You might as well stay now that Mary is not here. I know you were only being tactful in giving us a day together".

"Oh, I am having such a terrific time that I feel guilty about all of this Shaun", she said apologetically.

"I don't see why you should, Mary is very understanding and I know she wants you to enjoy yourself".

It wasn't long before Mary was forgotten about, as far as Sally was concerned, she loved his company and 'his lovely country as he had put it.

He told her that Ulster has suffered from a chequered past. Its tribes were powerful and its chieftains vigorous and except for the incursions of the Danes and such freebooters as John de Courcy and Edward Bruce it was comparatively undisturbed by foreign invasion.

She didn't want to hear all this today, maybe some other time, today she wanted to forget about history lessons, to enjoy the sightseeing and most of all his company and to hear him laugh.

As they drove away from his home Shaun told her that Newry is said to have taken its name from the legend that St Patrick himself planted a yew tree by the banks of the river. No surviving buildings are directly associated with Ireland's patron saint, but an abbey on the east bank of the river was built a couple of centuries later. He parked the car and brought her through the Roman Catholic Cathedral, built in Tudor Gothic style in 1825 by Thomas Duff; she was fascinated.

As they stepped outside into the sunshine Shaun said, with a wry smile, "Just to balance things off I'll take you through the Protestant Cathedral situated in Armagh later on today".

Sally laughed, "And which are you then?".

Shaun lightheartedly put an arm around her shoulder.

"Now that would be telling!".

They went on to Warrenpoint for lunch; it was a small seaside town with a lively promenade and spectacular views over the golf course.

Later that day they called at the 'Bronte Homeland Centre', near Banbridge, the birthplace of Patrick, father of the Bronte sisters.

"Tomorrow I will show you one of my favourite places, Gortin Glens, near Omagh and will take you deep into the glens that could very easily be missed by the ordinary tourist. I could sit there for hours painting and not notice the time go by", he said.

Sally hadn't enjoyed herself so much in her life and the weekend flew by.

She had found it to be a green and beautiful province, with lakes galore. Shaun had such a love for all nature, still life to animal. She wondered if all artists had this devotion as Mary certainly possessed it; she could perceive colours in a fish that would have been overlooked if attention hadn't been drawn to them. As they walked along the lakeside they noticed dozens of frustrated and vexed drakes desperately pursuing a few irate lady ducks. "Not a chance for some, poor devils", said Shaun, "There is a preponderance of males in the duck population this year, I do hope this doesn't presage a drop in our duck population. They are such delightful and amusing creatures with their quacking, squabbling, preening and fussing. The children love them, they provide such a lot of pleasure".

Then there were the singing rivers like 'The Londonderry Aire' one of the best loved traditional songs in this part of Ireland. There had been beaches, coves to explore and historic treasures to admire.

As they stood facing each other in the airport, they both felt deflated, neither of them knowing what to say to alleviate the sadness of parting. Shaun, on impulse held out his arms to her and she longingly went into them. She closed her eyes in torment, as she cherished the wonderful feeling of closeness, knowing that they would never be this close again, then she moved slightly to press her cheek against his.

At that precise moment, Shaun looked beyond her and gazed into the accusing eyes of Ron Casey. He loosened his hold on the beautiful blond girl so abruptly that she almost tumbled over. His gaze followed the man's form as he went through into the departure lounge with a supercilious gait.

Mary spoke to Sally on the phone after the weekend and was delighted that everything had gone smoothly and that she had enjoyed herself.

"I do wish you had been there, Mary, it doesn't seem right that you have never yet visited Shaun's lovely home and I have".

"Oh, I'll get there eventually, I usually arrange to meet up with him in Donegal, I can kill two birds with one stone then, but you are indeed right, I will have to make an effort".

She and Shaun rang each other regularly and she was glad he made no further mention of coming to France, at least for the present, as she was very busy.

Keith had a relapse and would be taking more time off than had been originally anticipated, so she had to take on more responsibility. It was very tiring but the rewards were numerous. She was elated every time she got a new tenant or if she could successfully sort out current tenant's problems.

The time was flying by at such a rate, she could hardly believe that the monthly meeting was on Thursday.

In contrast to the last meeting, when it came to her review, Ron gave her fully fifteen minutes of his time.

He congratulated her on her continuing success at the Château De Montville and then went on to explain what was to be her change of scenery.

"We haven't had great success in selling off our properties in Florida. There are a substantial amount of assets tied up there. It has become increasingly pressing to get buyers for them. If we can succeed, it would prove useful in reducing debts in other parts of the company and will enable us to keep up our contributions to charity.

You are blessed with a good brain and tend to get the

right answer rather quicker, and more often, than most and I would like you to go out there for a few days. I am not asking you to sell these properties, only to cast a fresh eye over the situation and see if you can come up with any ideas that have eluded the people who are constantly in the thick of it. No offence to the sales staff, but sometimes one can't see the wood for the trees when too involved.

I had intended sending Keith along with you but due to his relapse, unfortunately, I will be joining you in this instance. Will it cause you any difficulty in being ready to leave on Monday?"

"I should be able to fall in with that as I have tomorrow to tidy up a few loose ends at the office" she said enthusiastically.

Todd dropped them off at Gatwick and wished them a good trip.

Mary was somewhat apprehensive as to how they would put in the time on the plane, as it was an eight hour flight, in such close proximity and was pleasantly surprised at how quickly it seemed to go by. It was quite enjoyable at times just to relax with the headphones on and listen to music.

Ron told her about the weekend he had spent in Donegal. Mary had heard a little from Katie, but when talking on the phone, one only gets an outline.

Kevin and Katie were moving into the Manor the following month. Alison would be released from her housekeeping duties and replaced by a daily help. John and Kevin would share the gardening with occasional local labour during the summer months. Alison was delighted with the arrangement and was looking forward to life in the cottage.

Ron pretended to sleep for the last hour of the flight. His mind was full of Corrina and the fiasco of his unconsummated marriage. When the guests had all dispersed and they had gone back to his flat in Kensington they both felt the anticlimax. He had been under great stress all day, for the significance of what he was doing had been with him from the moment he opened his eyes in the morning. He was, in fact, marrying on the rebound and was simply hoping for the best. For a few weeks before the marriage he wasn't even sure if she was having second thoughts also as she had become quiet and aloof, but nothing was ever voiced between them.

She flung her hat onto the bed and said sarcastically, "So he swept his new bride into his arms, then lustfully made mad passionate love to her!".

They faced each other, he couldn't very well reprimand her for the satirical outburst. Her skin shone translucently, her eyes begged him to touch her. He knew many men would have given anything to be in his present position but he could not lay a finger on her, either in love or rage. He could see the disappointment on her sad face, she was a woman sexually thwarted and stripped of her dignity.

She had expected some sort of reaction but when she got

none, grabbed her handbag and ran to the front door, then he heard it slam.

Four hours later she was brought home in a state of disarray by a couple who said that while drowning her sorrows, she had become rowdy. Never in a million years could he have imagined her to be other than an impeccable, shining example of womanhood with panache, but there before him was a drunken, slovenly unrecognisable female. Seeing her in that state brought him to his senses. He felt deep shame and sorrow then persuaded himself that his marriage was worth a try. He undressed her and tucked her into bed, wiped her face tenderly with a wet flannel and waited until she fell asleep before he left her.

The next morning they discussed the situation. He acknowledged the fact that although he thought the world of her the marriage had been accelerated beyond his control and if she was patient with him, he was sure everything would turn out alright.

She also accepted part of the responsibility as she had expedited the wedding, due to pressures from family and friends.

Mary fought to stay awake and stopped her head, just in time, from falling on Ron's shoulder.

They arrived at Orlando International Airport weary and fatigued. Ron decided that when he was more rested and had time to study the routes and tollways they would hire a car next day, so they took the limousine service laid on which drove them to the door of the Hilton Hotel at Lake Buena Vista.

They parted, arranged to meet at breakfast, and retired to their allocated rooms. The hotel was out of this world with the very latest of electronic technology, one didn't even have to switch on a light.

After breakfast they drove to the Springlawn development. The elegantly designed homes, each enjoying their own individually landscaped gardens, were situated in Kissimmee, by Lake Tohopekaliga, south of Orlando, away from the tourist hotels but within four miles of Disney World and well placed as a base for getting around all the other attractions of Orlando. For recreation there were three 18-hole championship golf courses within easy reach.

Mary had never seen such luxurious homes. They were of three different styles, a choice of two, three or four bedrooms. The four and some of the three had private pools but all had access to the large shared swimming pool, exclusive to residents.

All of the homes were equipped with deluxe appliances, all the features one would ever want for easy living. Solar panels were built-in to save money and help protect the environment. These panels were also used to heat the swimming pools and contributed towards the central heating.

As Mary stood in the middle of one of the gardens, she

looked up at the vast blue sky and it suddenly hit her. She said to Ron, "There is too much sky, we need trees, fast growing trees for shade. The low shrubs, lovely as they are, will never be anything other than ornamental".

"It is a very good point, I will call in the experts to find out about fast growing trees that would complement the surroundings", said Ron, then queried lightly, "Any other proposals going through that active brain".

"Not for the moment, but I'll think of some I'm sure", she laughed.

"Oh, I've thought of something", said Ron. "A playground for the children".

"Would the type of people buying these luxury bungalows have children? I would have thought they would more likely be in the middle-aged group".

"Ah, but middle-aged people have grandchildren, you know the little rascals that grandparents can't wait to have visit, then can't wait to be rid of".

"Very good", she said laughing, "Now, we are quits". They were behaving in a lighthearted mood, but knew that they would have to get down to some more important issues, and swiftly, if these beautiful homes were to sell.

They spent the day visiting other competitor's holiday homes to see if they could come up with some fresh ideas and over lunch jotted down some useful points.

If the price of the homes was felt by the prospective buyers to be particularly off putting, they could stress its advantages by demonstrating it together with competing, inferior homes. Each customer who objected to the price should be given the opportunity to visit other homes, which would give them confidence and all resistance to the price should disappear. The customer would then relate to the value rather than be price conscious.

The heat was tremendous and Mary was glad she had adorned her well cut stone shorts with a tan contrasting belt. He was also in shorts and tee shirt. Once, when in the car, she accidentally touched his strong brown leg with hers as she bent to pick up the brochure and quickly jumped away leaving a more than appropriate gap between them. Without smiling, he casually said, "I am not contaminated you know and I don't burn, so sit properly in your seat, as we have a lot of driving to do over the next few days".

She shifted disconcertedly back into a more comfortable position.

All of the Americans they came into contact with were so kind and friendly and went out of their way to assist them in any way they could. It took them a while to get used to their manner as generally they never seemed to pause for breath when they were talking.

After they had their evening meal they were lucky to meet up with an extremely nice couple who said they would take them around the various nightspots. There was a good selection of night life in Kissimmee and they had a marvellous time and a lot of fun. Ron kept a keen eye on Mary's drinking as he was only too aware she wasn't able to handle it.

Ron and Mary declined the couple's invitation to go on to the Emporium Dance Palace to dance into the early hours to live music and instead followed their directions to a Country and Western evening, where there was a young Irish singer making an appearance. The young man was delighted to sing personally requested songs from the group of listeners.

Ron asked Mary if there was a song she would like him to sing, but she declined, saying she was happy to listen to the other's requests. He then asked him to sing 'The Donegal Shore". She hadn't heard this particular Donegal song and waited intently to hear the words. The silver tongued young singer came over to their table and sung the song specially for them:

I know its not right, reminiscing tonight
Of days that are gone and returning no more
For the girl I dream of gave another her love
Far, far away on a Donegal shore

When she told me she loved him it hurt to the core
And I couldn't descend to be only her friend
But I can't help my dreams of what might have been
If I'd won her love on the Donegal shore.

Mary listened to the other verses and hung onto the singer's every word with an aching heart knowing that he requested it in memory of the time she once had his love, but he now loved another.

Ron paced his bedroom floor, just three doors away from the woman he loved, a pitiful state of a man, sickened by his loathsome thoughts of what might have been if he had let her drink to the extent she had wanted to. If it had not been for his vigilance, in her inexperience, she would have drank the sweet Californian wine without being attentive to the alcoholic content.

As he paced he couldn't help thinking of the man she loved, and whom she thought reciprocated that love. He could strangle the philandering Irish man for being unfaithful to her. Everything had gone wrong for them both, why couldn't there be more equilibrium in life?

It had been a bad decision on his part to stand in for Keith, he could have put it off until Keith was fit. On deciding to have Mary join his company, it had been his intention to avoid close contacts such as these but he had been a glutton for punishment and punishment he now had in abundance. His need for her was great but he was after all only flesh and blood, when he got back he would claim his conjugal rights. Life that was once so simple was now a mass of complications.

The following morning Mary had a memo delivered to her room stating that he had some matters of protocol to attend to in connection with the Springlawn development and to spend the day as she wished and he would see her in the evening.

She relaxed by the pool all morning, occasionally

swimming a few lengths in the cool refreshing water. Today her mind was full of memories that were crystal clear - the feather like touch of his hands caressing her body on Tory Island. She turned over onto her back and as she drifted down the centre of the pool, the water flapping gently over her white swimsuit, her body ached longingly for the one man she could never possess.

She dried herself vigorously before reaching for her briefcase and set about listing ten ways that would benefit the properties. They were simple adjustments but when added together would generate a substantial improvement and should contribute to arousing further interest in them. There was one further proposal up her sleeve and when she got the main points together she would put it in writing for him.

She walked along the pavement towards one of the restaurants renowned for good food, stopping once to buy a French newspaper off the stand. It was remarkable how she had adjusted to the French way of life. When in France, she very often bought an English paper, but when away from both, she preferred to read the French news.

The restaurant was pleasantly air-conditioned and shaded with a range of tropical plants. The waiter beamed as he placed her at a table and told her, if she wished, she could join the buffet queue for a starter. She had never seen such an extensive range of exotic fruits and vegetables. Finally she decided to have a fruit salad tossed with feta cheese and a yoghurt based salad dressing, well seasoned, healthy and low in calories.

She had a leisurely lunch savouring every bite, then read through the business section of the paper with interest and fingered through the rest of it scanning for anything of interest. The gossip column caught her eye and she immediately folded the paper back to read what was written.

The caption read:
'Property magnate's wife named in divorce petition'
Madame Jannine Guerrin has lodged with her solicitor, a petition of divorce for adultery against her husband Michel, naming the corespondent Madame Corrina Casey.

Mary couldn't believe her eyes. How did the gossip column get this rubbish? It certainly couldn't be true. Jannine had left Michel a month before he had ever set eyes on Corrina. She also knew that Ron had excused himself last night in order to ring home and she hadn't noticed any variation in his attitude when he came back to her. She felt bad about it and threw the evidence in the bin, even though it was unlikely that Ron would have noticed the entry as he couldn't read French.

There was no doubt about it, Michel had been smitten with Corrina, but even if there had been a crumb of truth in it, how could it have advanced so fast. She and Ron have only been married about six weeks, they should still be honeymooners.

Mary knew that although Ron had been willing to forsake Corrina a week before their marriage, he would obviously love her dearly now. She was his woman; the one who was waiting for him at home in the evenings and shared his bed.

When she met up with Ron in the evening Mary had decided to put the libellous rubbish the newspaper had printed out of her mind. He ordered the meal but was subdued and spoke without vigour on a few events of the day. Once she met his eyes to try and read him, but he looked away. When a guitarist tried to serenade them, he was downright rude to him. He definitely must have heard the news. Her heart went out to him, but there was nothing she could do about it. She tried to be pleasant but was snubbed. Then he apologised, "Mary, I am sorry, I guess I am not in the best of form today. When we are through with this meal I will leave you in peace".

It was just 9.00pm when he escorted her to her room. "I am sorry about this, Mary, but I hope to get on with some writing in my room. Will you be alright?"

"Yes, I have some work to get on with as well", she said.

She stood and watched him walk away lethargically. She wondered if he really desired solitude and on impulse, she called, "Ron!"

He turned around slowly and looked at her, then said, "Yes ?"

She walked down the wide corridor, stopped three feet from him and diffidently said, "Do you remember the night I held my arms out to you?".

"Of course I do, how could I ever forget".

"I held out my arms to you that night for comfort, because I had been dealt a severe blow. I want you to hold out your arms to me now, because I want to comfort you".

He looked searchingly at her with raised eyebrows, then stepped towards her, took her by the arm and escorted her back to her open bedroom door, guiding her inside, closing the door behind them.

"So you want to comfort me, in my adversity!", he said with a hint of mockery in his voice.

"N-not if you don't need it or don't want me to", she stammered.

With a slight grimace he held out his arms to her and she went into them. She gave in to the rare pleasure of being held close to him and felt his heart thump as his hard chest flattened her breasts through her flimsy blouse. He whispered in her ear, "You are ravishing!".

The closeness, together with his after shave cologne, went to her head. Foolhardy and reckless she provocatively sought his lips with hers and he kissed her demandingly as if starved of passion and she likewise.

He loosened his hold on her and said softly, "Was the kiss in the comforting bargain as well, or did that come as an extra, and if so, are there any other addendums on offer tonight?".

She felt herself being reduced to a quivering jelly. Tremors charged through her body as the sexual impact of his words hit her and she felt weak. Instinctively she pressed her body against him and they both became aflame with desire; his exploring tongue pressed through her parted lips, at the same time she felt his body strong and demanding against hers. As the sweet sensations continued unabated, a little voice in her head warned that soon they would reach the point of no return. She longed to surrender but decisively removed herself from his grasp. She required more than his casual sexual need of her; above all she wanted his love, which wasn't on offer.

She said, "Oh Ron, I am so sorry about the way everything has turned out for us".

He gathered her into his arms again tenderly, then with a hushed voice he said, "I failed you that night Mary, failed to pour oil on your troubled waters. If I had only known then that you needed comforting because of McGready; but you see, I never knew about it until I saw them at the airport".

"I didn't need comforting because of Shaun, it was an entirely different matter, but I don't know what you are talking about".

He kept silent, not knowing what to make of this. Did she really not know about the scoundrel that lacked integrity?

By now thoroughly confused, she persisted, "What about the airport and Shaun?"

"I saw him at the airport with a blond, they looked very

intimate".

"That would have been my friend Sally, Shaun was seeing her off. You made a disproportionate assumption", she retorted.

He looked down at her and decided not to pursue the matter. McGready was beguiling her, God help her. He wished she didn't love him, that man should be treated with the contempt he deserved. He was a person of no consequence and not worth a discussion.

They were still holding onto each other but with a six inch gap between their bodies. He wanted to close that gap once more but the bastard McGready, had yet again, caused him to lose vantage ground.

Adopting a defeatist attitude he dropped a kiss on her curls and said, "Thank you Mary, goodnight, sleep well", and left her.

Before they booked out of the hotel on their last day, Ron, being a tennis fanatic, went off in search of a partner for a game.

She sat in the shade watching him play. He moved gracefully stretching and flexing in perfect coordination. He played with supreme confidence and inspiration to beat the young tennis coach 7-5, 6-4, in an hour and a half. She had been captivated from start to finish. He came up wiping his face and neck with the towel and she was glad the expression in her eyes was indistinguishable behind her dark sunglasses. This man disturbed her and would go on disturbing her for the rest of her natural life.

When showered and changed, Ron said he would never be able to live it down with Katie and Kevin if he didn't show her the wonderful tourist attractions of Disney World, within easy distance.

They had only five hours to spare and had to make the most of it as there was so much to see and do. They took a fifteen minute train journey around the 98 acres of the park's rides and attractions. The Town Square was a lively place with stalls, Dixieland bands and Disney characters welcoming them. They thoroughly enjoyed the Hall of Presidents, with animated figures of the nation's past leaders delivering famous speeches. After visiting Fantasyland, Epcot Center World Showcase, they were exhausted. Ron caught her hand restraining her as she was making towards the Mickey Mouse Club and humorously said, "Are you going to come peacefully or do I have to use force?".

She followed sadly knowing she would never forget the lovely time she had spent here in Ron's company.

On the plane, Ron was in a state of relaxation, listening to music, while Mary scribbled some notes. He switched it off as she spoke.

"How is the financial state of the company?"

"Not in the good position we were before the recession, but still keeping our head above water".

"Are you still in a position to buy for investment?".

Ron answered, "Yes, certainly".

She handed over an advert draft that she had been working on and asked his opinion. It read:

ATTENTION PLEASE: All of you who dream of owning your very own luxury property in the sunshine state, but have been put off by the property slump.

We have come up with a shrewd and reliable way in which you can have that home of your dreams, it is HOME X CHANGE

Please phone Ron Casey to find out more about the unprecedented assistance on offer.

They discussed it in more detail, and Ron agreed that if they bought the houses now, at the bottom of the market, it would indeed be an investment, as prices had to come back.

"I think it is a splendid idea, Mary. Keith and I shall certainly give it a lot of consideration".

They arrived back into Gatwick exhausted, and both went their separate ways, Ron to his Kensington flat and Mary to a hotel.

He let himself in and gathered up a heap of mail from the front door, wondering why Corrina hadn't dealt with it. He soon discovered her note.

Ron 'Perhaps you read the gossip column in Le Soir yesterday morning naming me as corespondent in a petition for divorce by Jannine against Michel Guerrin. I admit I have seen Michel on numerous occasions, indeed he tried to persuade me to forego my marriage to you two weeks before we were married but as I thought I loved you I declined. However, I have come to the conclusion that our marriage was a mistake and consequently, with deep regret, I have decided to leave, for both our sakes. I do not intend to petition for a quickie divorce against you for sexual inaptitude, although I very well could. I intend going to Michel as I know he loves me and within a week you should have your grounds for divorce'. Corrina.

On looking round the flat he satisfied himself that she had in fact gone. Yes, lock, stock and barrel. He sat down in daze but was amazed at the relief he felt. His marriage had turned out to be a pain and he wished her well. As for himself, life would be less complimented. Kevin hadn't needed women all those years, likewise he would manage very well without them. He would seek an annulment straight away.

Mary must have read the Le Soir newspaper and misjudged his despondency that evening had been due to his marriage problems. He had also wrongly assumed that as he had requested a love song reminiscing about their split in Donegal she had been sorry for him because of her love for McGready. He should have known better, but beggars can't be choosers, they accept any crumb on offer. As he relived the glorious feeling of her lips on his, giving and taking lips, he wondered how a woman could give so passionately without loving - obviously she could. God forbid that any woman would ever hold him in their arms again for pity. If he ever felt the physical need, he would not deny himself.

He went to the drinks cabinet and poured himself a double Scotch and before downing it, held out the glass and said aloud, "Devil take the hindmost! To hell with regard for teasing women or self respect".

He was on his fourth double when he said sluringly, "To hell with women who filled the cupboards with superfluous things like bleach and made you drink today's milk tomorrow".

Mary received an early call to go to the Hilton Hotel where a room had been booked by the sales staff promoting the Springlawn homes. She was exhausted as she made her way across London, she had been on edge and had slept very little.

Her eyes fell on Ron straight away as she entered the seminar. He was dressed in a charcoal suit and crisp white shirt and colourful tie. He looked fatigued but as usual put on a good front as he gave a short presentation. He had been unprepared for this, but carried the situation on hand superbly, absolutely unflappable. She caught his last words, "Our jet lagged Miss Lavery will be at your disposal for first hand advice".

He stood aside and spoke to a promising customer but was aware of Mary constantly. She looked enchanting in a fresh pink linen suit and cream silk blouse and had acquired a tan during her time in Florida. Mingling with the crowd of prospective buyers she moved easily, without apparent haste; her voice came to his ears serenely as he heard her deciphering, offering information and commenting on different aspects of the holiday homes. Suddenly his thoughts sent a shiver through him as he knew he must remain steadfast in his intention of last evening.

The session was progressing encouragingly; he drew her aside and asked her to see him in his office at 12.30.

Mary entered his office smiling haughtily. Her smile died and she became faintly disturbed when she observed his sombre expression.

"Sit down, Mary!", said Ron, indicating to the chair.

She noted his melancholy and tension as he drummed the fingers of his left hand on the desk.

Their eyes met and locked as he said, "I am sorry, Mary, there is no easy way to put this to you, but I have decided to release you from your duties herewith. I think you will find this cheque more than generous, particularly as you have only been with the company for a very short period of time".

Mary couldn't believe her ears, it was the last thing on this earth she had expected to hear. She had left the seminar in an elevated mood, happy that the sales meeting had gone well. Other than Ron's love there was nothing she wanted more than her job; she lived for it, now, in one sickening sweep, he was stripping her of everything including her dignity. She had undoubtedly boosted sales and felt very happy working here, working well in a team with Keith as well as the rest of the staff and couldn't think of any other people she would prefer working with. It was not as if she had made a hotchpotch of the job, to the contrary, she had given the company one hundred per cent dedication. Now, for a figure on a cheque, he wanted her to concede defeat while he turned her career and motivation for living to dust.

The cheque lay face up, moving her fingers towards it, turned it over, she wasn't going to read it. He couldn't get away with it, she would take a firm stance in defiance of him.

"You can't get away with doing this to me, Ron, I was under the impression that we had a mutual respect for each other professionally and that our old problems were behind us. I can do this job, and do it well, without being joined to you by the hip. Everything was going fine until Keith became ill and couldn't accompany me on a few occasions". She paused for breath, then continued, "The law is on my side, Ron, I won't take this lying down, it is unequivocal unfair dismissal and I am determined to..."

He stopped her before she could voice her intention, saying, "I know you are a woman of determination, but I advise you not to go down that road, it could be nasty".

"Nasty for you, you mean!", she replied with acridity.

She felt like continuing with a barrage of hostile criticism but thought better of it and attempted to assume the stance of a woman in control of the situation. She said calmly, "No cheque can buy silence, Ron, and I shall do what I have to do".

As she was letting herself out of the office door, he called, "For Christ's sake take the damn cheque, it is worth more than a court would award you for unfair dismissal".

She closed the door without faltering for a second.

Karen heard her mutter, "Damn him, damn his cheque!", as she hurried past completely oblivious of her existence.

Chapter Twelve

Mary tried one further time to call Shaun, but he still wasn't answering the phone in person. His voice was coming over the answer phone, "Sorry I'm not home, please leave a message". This time she left a message - "Mary speaking, I'm going home to Katie, arriving 11.30am Aldergrove. If possible meet me for an hour".

Much as she had tried, she just couldn't keep the impersonality out of her voice. She didn't know what to make of Ron's disclosure regarding Shaun and Sally. She would check out the facts and if there was any truth in it, would recede in a dignified manner.

Was she able to cope with this type of betrayal? More importantly, did she really care?

She had neglected Shaun, leaving him vulnerable to the temptation of an accommodating woman. No! She could not blame him, or Sally for that matter, proximity breeds attraction.

Shaun deserved someone like Sally, who would shower him with love and devotion, whereas she herself, would give devotion in abundance but could never supply the love.

The plane arrived in but there was no sign of Shaun. She had arranged for Kevin and Katie to pick her up at 1.00pm, so that if Shaun had got her message, they would have had an hour together. She hadn't felt well during the flight so went to the lounge and ordered an orange juice. Her head throbbed and her throat ached. She could hear her name being called, "Would Miss Mary Lavery, please go to ... ".

Shaun had put out the call for Mary at the airport and had been waiting patiently for her to respond when he spied her being carried on a stretcher by the airport ambulance staff. He accompanied her to the hospital after leaving a message for Kevin and Katie.

The obscure virus she had picked up in America was difficult to treat. She drifted in and out of consciousness for two weeks, during which time she had visions of people coming and going; just as she was about to touch them, they disappeared into thin air.

In the haziness, she sensed his closeness. Her desire for him was inflamed and she became consumed by it. Lights twinkled and sparkled as she held out her arms and drew him to her. She felt his firm body against hers, demandingly. She succumbed willingly to an overbearing passion as she was carried along on the increasing waves of euphoria.

"Mary! Mary!".

She whispered his name passionately in response and at long last opening her eyes... and looked into the anxious gaze of Shaun.

She stayed a further two weeks in hospital before being allowed home.

In the month that followed, Shaun devoted the best part of his time to her, seriously neglecting his work. He stayed with Alison and John, where he took possession of his old bedroom.

Kevin, Katie and Shaun, collectively, helped her through her illness and to regain her spirit which had ebbed due to her involuntary change of status.

As she regained her strength, Shaun encouraged her to start painting and they spent some relaxing days together painting more of the Donegal countryside, where the mountains were ever present and the sea prowled through many inlets.

For Mary it was a voyage of discovery, the images around them were consistently fantastic and the painting had a therapeutic effect on her.

On their expeditions, Shaun never failed to add his knowledge and history of the areas they were painting. He took her to Doe Castle near Creeslough. The MacSweeneys settled there in 1440 and it apparently was occupied until 1890. It was protected by the sea on three sides and by deep fosse on the fourth, which was spanned by a bridge. It was surrounded by a lawn around which was a curtain wall punctuated by towers. On the tower is an interesting tomb slab originally erected in the nearby graveyard to the memory of a MacSweeney. Shaun had painted this castle on previous occasions but never failed to find a new angle to paint from.

On another occasion they went to Milford near the head of

Mulroy Bay, a beautiful glen, very popular in the locality and adorned by two waterfalls.

The peaceful hours they shared in each others company were near an end as Shaun had a presentation to attend in London. They went for a drive locally to the lake at Falcarragh and to the edge of the pier. He turned off the engine and wound down the window while they sat silently watching the fishermen haul in the live lobsters. He had made no demands on her since her illness and the extent of their physical amour was to hold hands contentedly. Laying his elbow on the steering wheel, he turned to her. She was the picture of health, her face reflected the bracing freshness of the Donegal air.

He said hesitatingly, "I have been tolerant for such a long time, Mary, but unfortunately I am not blessed with the patience of Job. I know your job was very important to you and the illness was an unfortunate setback, but I never intended that we should have a long engagement and we both know the time is long overdue for discussing our future plans".

She dropped her eyes to avoid his gaze. Her illness had caused her to take a philosophical attitude to more things than one. Her main failure was that she had let Ron off lightly for treating her so callously. However, the matter in hand needed to be dealt with tactfully, she couldn't endure it if she were to lose Shaun's friendship. She unhappily twisted the ring off her finger, "I love you Shaun, but I am not in love with you, you deserve more than I can give".

His Irish temperament reared its ugly head as he flung the ring with accelerated force through the open window; it bounced twice along the quay before disappearing into the dark, murky depths of the water.

He sat back into the seat of the car dejectedly and said through pursed lips, "I think I have known the extent of your feelings for me all along. It's him, isn't it? It's always been him!".

"Unfortunately, yes", she sighed through trembling lips.

"The worthless cad, I fail to understand the mentality of that man. He won your love but cast it aside to marry someone else; he then had the audacity to entice you with an over elaborate job; when you succeeded beyond expectations, the bloody blackguard sacked you. I swear to God, Mary, I'll knock him for six if I ever get the chance". His voice was just short of a bellow as he uttered the last sentence.

She very quickly retorted, "You don't understand Shaun!".

"I understand enough to know that the bastard has made you unbearably unhappy". Then he quietly added, "The only thing you uttered when you were delirious was 'Ron' time and time again".

"I'm sorry, Shaun! I'll get over him. As you say, he's a bastard".

Shaun looked at her in disbelief: Christ! Now the bastard

had her swearing.

They got out of the car and walked along the fine golden sand. The place was almost deserted except for a few people wandering in the distance. She slid her fingers into his hand and wished they could be friends for ever. She was first to speak, "Ron told me that he saw you and Sally together and that it looked very intimate".

"The cad, I bet he couldn't wait to tell you that. I admit that Sally and I had a good weekend together and when the time came to part, it was sad - that was all".

Mary stopped walking, turned to him and said, "Promise me you won't lose touch with Sally, I know she thinks the world of you?".

"I promise", he said with a hint of a smile, "All she wanted that weekend was to enjoy the grand tour of the province, so I still owe her a history lesson".

With a lump in her throat Katie sadly watched Shaun and Mary embrace before he got into the car and drove off. She knew they would both occupy a special place in each other's hearts and the broken engagement was for the best.

She never knew what happened between Ron and Mary, but it was obvious that Mary had been deeply hurt. In the early days of the delirium, Ron's name was forever on her lips, oscillating from loving to hating him. Shaun had suffered an embittered torment in those days as he never left her side.

Eventually Ron had written to Mary, in Donegal, after Kevin told him of her illness. It had been a very short sympathetic note with a cheque enclosed for services rendered. Mary had cried uncontrollably when she received it. Katie's heart had gone out to her at the finality of it all.

Ron kept away while Mary was here, if he had a weekend to spare he went to visit Belinda, but by reading the papers they knew a more encouraging picture was emerging for his company. Among the tit-bits, they read that the Château De Montville was now fully occupied and sales of his Florida homes had taken off after they adopted a property exchange programme.

The Manor was now furnished to Katie's preference, but Kevin decided that Ron's bedroom should be left untouched. Katie ran the Manor efficiently, expensively and admirably. She was a new woman, entertained Lucy and Jock Watson and a host of others with the greatest of pleasure and ease. She succeeded in encouraging Mary to make herself at home and move easily throughout the house and respected her wish not to enter Ron's room.

Mary loved the Manor almost as much as Katie and she shared a very close relationship with Kevin. They enjoyed long cheerful conversations together in the garden but she remained steadfast in keeping the secret of parentage from him, much to Katie's chagrin.

Kevin laid the morning paper aside, unopened, as he

joined Katie and Mary at the breakfast table. Mary leaned over to observe the picture on the front page of two men having a brawl and a blond girl trying to intervene.

"My God!", she gasped, as she drew the paper closer. The picture was of Shaun and Ron. Shaun had obviously hit Ron as he was in the process of bringing back his fist. Ron was on his way down and Sally was clutching Shaun's jacket as if to restrain him.

The caption read:
'Artist McGready, hits out in Tug of Love'.
Shaun McGready, the highly acclaimed artist, last night knocked Ron Casey, the property tycoon, to the ground after a hostile confrontation outside a London Theatre. The attractive blond, in the centre of the conflict, who remains unknown, left McGready to call a taxi and accompany Mr Casey to hospital. Casey, recently divorced, received treatment for a deep gash on the forehead, for which he received three stitches. When asked later, if he wanted to press charges for the assault, Casey said, 'No! I will not be taking proceedings against him'.

Katie picked up the teapot and disconcertedly poured the tea. She was ghostly white, praying for a miracle to rid them of this curse her sister had put on them.

Kevin was awe-struck but managed to ask, "Do any of you know the girl they were fighting over?"

"Yes, she is my friend, Sally", said Mary, "But I don't know if she had anything to do with it; they just hate each other..."

Katie stopped her saying anything further by butting in with, "Lets not surmise without the facts".

Sally rang Mary later in the morning to explain the news report. "It's strange how those damn reporters and photographers crawl out of thin air at the slightest whiff of a scandal. I may have a soft spot for Shaun but I can assure you I am not after Ron".

"I know you are not after Ron, but why should it worry me if you were?", asked Mary cautiously.

Sally ignored the question and went on to say, "Shaun is taking it very badly today after hitting Ron last night. You see I told him later that Ron was not the one to terminate the short relationship you had together, that it had been, in fact, you. In all the time I have known Shaun, he detested Ron Casey and avoided speaking of him, now he is actually sorry for the guy".

"Thank you for ringing me, Sally, and whatever you do don't let Ron Casey ruin the time you and Shaun have together, he isn't worth it. Probably at this very moment he will be riding roughshod over some other poor unsuspecting mortal".

Katie and Mary were quietly tidying up the kitchen, neither of them referring to the incident, although it was uppermost in each of their thoughts, when there was a sudden screech of brakes outside in the drive. The door flung open and in walked Ron. Mary's heart missed a beat and she could feel herself go white as a sheet as she stared at his unshaven face, an ugly gash on his forehead and one black eye. She hadn't set eyes on him since he had sat across the office from her and delivered that fatal debilitating blow.

"Mary", he said, ignoring Katie, "Do you love me?".

It was a simple, direct question, but he threw it at her accusingly.

Katie held unto the table for support as she lowered herself into the seat.

"Yes, damn you!", Mary answered.

Katie raised both her hands and face to the ceiling and cried in despair, "God have mercy upon us!".

Ron caught Mary by the wrist and drew her out of the kitchen, dragged her the whole way down the garden and into the summer house, where he turned her round to face him.

"If you love me, why did you wreck my life?".

Mary looked him straight in the eyes as she answered him, "I discovered Kevin was my father".

"Oh, my God, the eyes. In this very garden on that first night, and on occasions since, I knew those unusual eyes reminded me of someone but couldn't think who". He drew her into his arms and held her tightly, she sighed with relief as she pressed her smooth face against his stubble.

Without loosening his hold on her he moved his head back to look into her eyes as he said, "I have been driving all night to catch the ferry to Ireland, sorry about the stubble!", then quickly asked, "Darling, why didn't you tell me that night in France when I told you that Jack was my father?".

"By that time, the whole gabit of events had taken over. The last thing I wanted to do was hurt Shaun, also there was Corrina, you were within a week of getting married".

"I never thought I'd thank Shaun McGready for anything, but he did me a great favour when he punched me". It was the first time Mary had heard Ron call Shaun by his christian name.

"When I saw him laughing with the blond girl, I went up to him and called him a two timing rat. He caught me by the scruff of the neck - I'll never forget his strength as he dragged me outside and landed one on me. Funny enough, it was his words that astounded me and had the greater impact. In his broad Irish accent he bellowed at me, 'You bloody filthy scum, she gave you her unmerited love and you threw it back in her face, as if that wasn't enough you then took great pride in demoralising her by throwing her on the scrap heap'".

Mary's eyes wandered to the gash on his forehead and smilingly said, "Well, it looks as if you and Shaun will have one thing in common after all".

"I don't know what his feelings are towards Sally, but she certainly is in love with him and on the way to the hospital she conveyed that she intuitively thought that you were in love with me", said Ron.

"Sally and Shaun will remain my friends for ever, which might mean one day you may have to succumb to shaking Shaun by the hand", Mary said hopefully.

"Very well, I will shake his hand vigorously as long as I am assured that he loves Sally and not you, after all he opened my eyes to the truth".

Mary was hopeful of that day arriving and in the not too distant future.

She disentangled herself, saying urgently, "We had better go in, Katie will be out of her mind".

Ron pulled her into his arms again and kissed her; Katie was forgotten as she clung to him for dear life.

"Mary, my darling you have no idea the agonies I went through when you were ill, wanting to be with you so much but knowing he was watching over you and thinking that was what you wanted".

"Shaun was there for me, but I wanted only you", she whispered as she held him closer.

With memories of the night they came back from Tory Island, when they were deliriously happy and had declared their love for each other, Ron murmured against her lips,

"Mary, will you marry me very quickly? I am so scared of you dreaming up some reason why we can't be together".

Mary teased him, "Well, only if I can have my job back".

"No chance!", he laughed, "You'd do better sticking with your painting, I want the benefit of my wife's advice without having to employ her".

Nothing mattered to Ron - recessions, successful sales or setbacks. All that mattered was that he could once again hold her in his arms and that she was eager to hold him in return. As they kissed passionately once again the immense aggravations and jadedness of the past weeks took flight.

Katie and Kevin were standing in the garden as they approached. Katie looked very worried, she had never seen Mary and Ron look so happy, as they laughed together with their arms around each other.

"Don't worry, Aunt Katie, everything is going to be alright", said Mary.

Ron confronted Kevin with the words, "Do you want the bad news or the good news first?".

"Well", said Kevin thoughtfully, "I wouldn't like to die of a heart attack at the bad news before I had a chance of hearing the good news".

"The good news is, Mary is your daughter. The bad news

is you are going to be stuck with me as a son in law and that Jack was in fact my father".

They all cried with happiness as they embraced each other in turn.

"Glasses! Katie, get the good glasses! Sure if ever that 1976 champagne deserved poppin', 'tis today", said Kevin excitedly.

Katie, happier than she had ever been, was in the process of embracing Ron, pressed her soft cheek against his stubble, said bossily, "Not a drop of champagne goes through Ron's lips till he gets rid of this bristle".

She then linked arms with Kevin and they walked towards the Manor ahead of Ron and Mary.

Mary whispered to Ron, as they followed, with a half-shy expression, "I can't wait to share your eighteenth century four poster bed".

He held her tightly against him as he murmured in response, "Let's hope we won't have too long to wait for that - we will see about a special marriage licence today".

* * *

Ron handed the contented bundle to Katie and went back to sit on the bed close to Mary where she was still flushed from the traumas of giving birth and the excitement of owning their very own two hour old baby.

Katie held the baby close and smiled at Kevin as she said, "She has her grandfather's eyes".

Kevin put his index finger into the tiny hand and the baby gripped it tightly, then he asked, "Has this little girl got a name yet?".

"Yes," replied Ron, "She will be christened Susan Belinda, after both of her grandmothers'".

Katie's eyes lit up with happiness and a tear came tumbling down and splashed on the child's face, Sue should not be forgotten at a time like this nor her words '*...for it to run and play on the beautiful Tranarossan sands and scurry over the rocks at Marble Hill. I want it to frequent Rosguill, Horn Head, MacSwiney's Gun at Trawmore and...*'

Kevin and Katie left: Katie's excited voice could be heard as they made their way down the hospital corridor. "I want you to design me a dream cottage with roses round the door, sure the Manor needs the patter of tiny feet and..."

Ron and Mary smiled happily at each other as Katie's excited voice receded.

"Do you want to hold your baby?", Ron asked as he tenderly smoothed back a stray lock of hair from her forehead.

"I want you! But our baby will do to be going on with".

He placed the baby in Mary's arms. She was very, very tired and with closed eyes she whispered soothingly, "Sue, I'm going to take you to a little bridge that a lot of water has run under since I was last there and I'll catch a little minnow for you, maybe two, with my bare hands".

Ron replaced the baby in its cot; Mary needed some sleep - sure she was raving.